Dra

Ch

Dragonology
Chronicles
⋇ VOLUME FOUR ⋇

THE DRAGON PROPHECY

Dugald A. Steer

illustrated by Nick Harris

CANDLEWICK PRESS

Copyright © 2012 by Dugald A. Steer
Illustrations copyright © 2012 by Nick Harris

First U.S. edition 2012

Library of Congress Cataloging-in-Publication Data is available.
Library of Congress Catalog Card Number pending

ISBN 978-0-7636-3428-5

12 13 14 15 16 17 BVG 10 9 8 7 6 5 4 3 2 1
Printed in Berryville, VA, U.S.A.

This book was typeset in Granjon.

Candlewick Press
99 Dover Street
Somerville, Massachusetts 02144

visit us at www.candlewick.com

For Georgina and Jimmy

D. S.

For the team at Templar

N. H.

PROLOGUE

The man lay facedown on the beach where the storm had left him. Mountainous waves had broken over his fishing boat, smashing the rudder, and hurricane winds had driven her towards the baleful shore. They had come upon land in the evening. But what land? There was no record of it on any chart. It had appeared out of the night, its black cliffs vanishing upwards into the driving rain and the darkness. The men had smelled a curious stench of sulphur mixed with that of sea wrack, but hadn't had time to ponder it. The waves had dragged the boat out to safety only to slam her back against the shore, where the shock of collision sent the crew tumbling across the deck like marbles. One by one the men had slid overboard, as the boat's tortured hull finally snapped in two and a wave washed over the gunnels to swamp her. Only one man was swept to safety. It was a miracle. He could not move, so he slept.

The man awoke in bright sunshine. Above him was the overhang of a cliff, beyond which a number of large birds wheeled and dived, so high as to be nearly out of sight. He began to climb, and, once he had scaled the overhang, although the jagged rocks were sharp and cut his chafed hands, his ascent grew easier. Halfway up he caught another whiff of sulphur—it reminded him of rotten eggs. When he reached the top of the cliff, he discovered the reason for the smell. This land was an island, and in the centre, surrounded by dense jungle, was a smoking volcano. There were distant sounds—booms and cracks—that the man could not identify. He glanced up at the creatures circling the volcanic peak. Now that he could see them more clearly, he realised that they were not birds at all. For which bird had a scaly tail or wings like a giant bat? Despite his predicament, his heart beat with sudden excitement: had he discovered a lost island where dinosaurs still roamed?

A winged creature about a foot long zigzagged among the rocks towards him. It fixed the man with its beady eyes and hovered for a moment, as though challenging him to follow, before it turned tail and vanished. It wasn't so much a dinosaur as a tiny dragon. The man picked up a rock and set off in the direction the creature had gone. He crested a rise, and the scene that met him made his jaw drop in astonishment. Before him lay a vast pit filled with enormous dragons, some harnessed to large carts surrounded by teams of toiling humans. As he watched, a huge white dragon breathed searing frost onto a rock face, then a black dragon spewed out fire so hot that the rock shattered, spilling rubble that the men shovelled onto the carts.

"Are you entertained by this display, stranger?"

The female voice spoke English with the slightest trace

of a foreign accent. The man spun round to behold a beautiful, black-haired woman, cradling in her arms the small dragon that he had been following. Behind her a party of armed men stood, as though awaiting her orders.

The man gestured towards the pit. "I never believed in dragons until now," he said. "Is it right to force them to work?"

The woman bit her lip and scowled. "How dare you!" She paused, then smiled and stroked the top of the small dragon's head. "They make elephants work. I need these dragons to help me find something that was lost. Something very precious that was hidden long ago." The dragon stretched out in her arms like a cat. "Searching is hungry work, is it not, Flitz?" She looked steadily at the man. "My poor dragons are always hungry." The woman turned to her guards. "Take him to the pit!" she commanded. "We will find a use for him — one way or another."

As the guards led the man away, the sound of the woman's laughter echoed among the rocks.

CHAPTER ONE
THE HIGHLANDS
OF SCOTLAND

When in the field, the student of dragonology should let neither
the hottest desert sandstorms nor the iciest Arctic blizzards
discourage him: he must be a dragonologist for all seasons.

—— *Dr. Ernest Drake, Letters to a Young Dragonologist*

R ain had smudged the edges, and water was puddling
in the heart-shaped pad, but to the practised eye, the
dragon clawprint was unmistakable. The foreclaws had left
three long, light impressions, while the single hind claw
had gouged a deep hole in the wet sand. I stood up quickly
and beckoned to my sister, then squatted down again out
of sight. Beatrice's skirt dragged across the ground like a
wet mop, and her boots squelched noisily as she crept alongside me.

"How could I have missed that?" she exclaimed, shaking her head.

"I think it's still fresh," I said.

"It doesn't look fresh. The edges have fallen in."

"That's the rain." I pointed to the middle of the print. "It can't have been here long or the pad would have filled up with water."

Beatrice bent down to examine the track more closely. "It's not close by, Daniel. I can't smell sulphur."

I knew the pungent odour of dragons as well as Beatrice did, and she was right. Now that we had found the first clawprint, it was easy to see a line of them, showing where the dragon had walked along the footpath for about fifty yards before heading into the trees on the right. I touched Beatrice's shoulder. "Why do you think a dragon risked leaving tracks on a footpath?"

"Perhaps it thought they would get washed away."

"More probably it's a trap and it's waiting to ambush us," I said.

We left the path and made our way carefully uphill through the trees, following a trail of flattened heather. A pine trunk bore fresh scratches where the dragon had stopped to sharpen its claws before climbing onwards onto the scrubby grass and bare rock of the mountain peak. Here the rain had turned to whirling snow, and there was no protection from the bitter wind. I saw something flying overhead and fumbled for my binoculars.

"It's not a dragon, is it?" said Beatrice.

"No, it's a buzzard. I can see the stripes on its tail. But what is it doing out in this weather?"

It wasn't long before we came across a pile of bloody

bones and a torn fleece. It was the remains of a predator's meal, and judging by the incisor marks on the skull — which had been cracked open like a walnut — it was obviously the work of a dragon. Beatrice bent over the remains and placed a hand on the fleece. As soon as she touched it, she pulled her hand back and let out a gasp.

"What are you doing?" I cried.

"The fleece is freezing," said Beatrice. "I expected it to be warm, yet from the look of it, the dragon has only just finished eating."

Gingerly, I lifted up the fleece. It was frozen so solid that I felt like I was picking up a thick sheet of ice.

"The effects of a frosty blast!" said Beatrice knowingly.

I nodded. As I looked up, I spotted a dark opening in the cliffs beneath the summit of the rapidly whitening mountain.

"Look, Bea!" I said. "A cave mouth!"

Beatrice dropped into a crouch, pulling me down with her. "Let's find out if anyone's at home," she whispered. We worked our way along the bottom of the cliff, keeping the blizzard at our backs, and found another, larger pile of bones. A strong reek of sulphur confirmed this to be a dragon's lair. I felt my heart begin to thud.

"Did you bring any treasure?" I whispered hopefully.

Beatrice shook her head anxiously. "I thought you said you were going to bring the treasure this time."

"I couldn't find anything." I shot her a guilty look.

Beatrice folded her arms. "What about your dragon whistle? This could be a matter of life or death!"

My hand felt for the thick chain around my neck. My dragon whistle had been a precious gift from the Master of Hong Wei Temple in China. I would do anything rather than give it away. Beatrice had been given her own whistle, but there was no chance she would give hers up. Not when I was supposed to have provided the treasure. . . .

I thought for a moment, then an idea came to me.

"I'm going to ask it a riddle," I said.

"In English . . . or Dragonish?" Beatrice said warily. She knew that my Dragonish wasn't a patch on hers.

"In English," I said firmly. I strode off towards the crack in the cliff and coughed to let the dragon know that I was there. From deep inside the cave, I heard a stifled roar — but it wasn't the full, deep roar that I was expecting. To my surprise, I heard an old gentleman's voice whisper, "Shhh, Torcher!" I shot a glance at Beatrice, to find that she was staring openmouthed at the sky. I spun around just in time to see a winged shadow fall across the ground as Erasmus, our dragon tutor, landed in a maelstrom of snowflakes. He folded his wings together over his back, gave us a withering look, and let out a loud sigh.

"Dead!" he exclaimed, flicking his tail irritably. "You are both dead! Why can't you get it right? Let us go inside."

It was a relief to be in a warm, dry cave out of the terrible weather. Dr. Ernest Drake — whose voice we had

heard, and from whom we had learned pretty much all the dragonology we knew — was waiting for us by a fire with a hot drink and an encouraging smile. Meanwhile, Torcher, the dragon chick that we had raised from his egg, sent us both flying, in his rush to greet us. Erasmus, still shaking his head, snaked his white body through the entrance crack and sat back on his scaly haunches.

"Do you call that a performance fit for a pair of first-class dragonologists?" he scoffed. "If I were a hungry frost dragon and we had not been introduced, the buzzard that was flying around down there would be feasting on the remains of two foolish children by now."

"Come now, Erasmus," said Dr. Drake. "Their technique is not perfect, but it is extremely good. Do not be too hard on them."

Erasmus let out a dismissive snarl. "Hard on them?" he roared. "Of course I have to be hard on them! These children have been selected to train for the ultimate position available to human dragonologists: the role of Dragon Master. What use will either of them be if they get themselves slaughtered and eaten the first time they meet one of my relatives?"

"What did we do wrong?" I asked.

"I should have thought that was obvious," said Erasmus dryly. "First, you did not see me fly from the cave while you were busy poking around in the remains of my lunch. You should have wondered why the buzzard made itself scarce so quickly. And then, to avoid getting snow in your faces, you chose to approach my cave from upwind! Any animal could smell you a mile away. I shall inform Idraigir that I am finished with you. I can no longer be tutor to two such useless pupils! Dragon school is over!"

And with that, Erasmus disappeared out of the cave, his long tail flicking from side to side.

"Do you think he really means it?" asked Beatrice anxiously.

"Of course not," replied Dr. Drake. "Idraigir will not permit your training to come to an end. Erasmus has too much to learn about humans."

"He obviously doesn't like what he's learned so far," I muttered.

Dr. Drake smiled ruefully. "That may be true, but Erasmus's frost dragon relatives are the real reason he's upset. In fact, that is why I have come here. I am afraid I need your help."

CHAPTER TWO

A MYSTERY

The Earth turning on its axis, summer following spring,
night following day and the twice-yearly migration of the frost
dragons: at one time I believed that they were all as unstoppable
as my own greedy hunger for knowledge.

—— *Dr. Ernest Drake, Letters to a Young Dragonologist*

Back at the hunting lodge, we changed out of our damp clothes and warmed ourselves in front of a roaring fire in the grand drawing room. Dr. Drake spread out a series of maps on a long table by the window, and we sat down to examine them with our mother and father. Each map had a title, such as *Spring 1874* or *Autumn 1880,* and each bore an illustration of the entire world, crisscrossed with red and black arrowed lines and annotated with numerous hand-written place-names and dates.

"What do the lines show?" I asked.

"Can't you guess, Daniel?" said Mother. She pointed to one particular place-name: Jaisalmer, in the north of India.

"Father and I made these observations." She sounded very proud of the fact.

Beatrice was smiling. "I know what they are," she said. "These are maps of frost dragon sightings during their two migrations each year."

"Well done, Beatrice," said Dr. Drake. "I have brought these maps here to illustrate our problem. These examples cover the last ten years, but the Secret and Ancient Society of Dragonologists has similar maps stretching all the way back to 1823. As you can see, the number of sightings has increased every year, until we get to this latest map."

He held it up. At the top it was marked *Autumn 1883*. "But there aren't any sightings on that one at all," I said.

"That is our problem in a nutshell, Daniel. Usually reports of sightings are pouring in to the S.A.S.D. headquarters by now, via coded telegram. Dragon Man Dan always tries to be the first to make a sighting from the Blue Mountains in Australia. But this autumn he hasn't spotted a thing. It is as though the migration has simply not taken place — which is, of course, impossible."

By this time, Father was pacing the room, his hands folded behind him under the long tails of his jacket. I knew he felt that the recent extinction of the naga dragons in India was somehow his responsibility, even though there was nothing he could have done. Perhaps he was afraid the same thing might now be happening to the frost dragons. "Can I mention her?" he said ominously.

"Alexandra Gorynytchka?" asked Dr. Drake. "Yes, of course. I cannot deny that I immediately suspected her involvement in this mystery. I always knew we had not seen the last of that woman. I asked Idraigir to contact the other intelligent dragons via the Dragon Vine to ask for news of Miss Gorynytchka, but so far no one has heard a peep from her. It is almost as though Miss Gorynytchka — like the frost dragons — has vanished into thin air."

My father thumped a fist on the table. "Well, they must be somewhere!"

"Excuse me, but what is the Dragon Vine?" I asked.

"It is like the Dragon Express," replied my father, running his fingers through his hair anxiously. "It is a way in which intelligent dragons pass on information they consider useful to other dragons around the world." He turned to Dr. Drake. "What does Erasmus say about the frost dragons?"

"Erasmus is extremely upset about it, and who could blame him? Idraigir has agreed to let him fly south, to see if he can find out what has happened to his kinsfolk. I have asked Idraigir to explore the north, while Brythonnia and Tregeagle will search east and west."

"What would you like us to do?" asked Beatrice eagerly.

"From now on, I want you to keep watching the skies, day and night. It will be best if you take turns."

"Do you really think that we'll be able to spot a frost dragon if no one else has?" I asked.

"I believe that you have a sporting chance. Frost dragons

are exceptionally cautious creatures and have very little to do with any other species of dragon. However, there is a possibility that if they are in trouble, then one of them will come here seeking Erasmus; he is the son of their leader, after all. So keep your eyes peeled. And keep Torcher with you. He has the best eyesight of all."

As if he were demonstrating the truth of Dr. Drake's words, I saw that Torcher was standing on his hind legs at the window, watching something with great intensity.

"What is he looking at out there?" asked my father.

"It's Erasmus," said my mother, crossing the room towards the little dragon. "And he is approaching at considerable speed."

Dr. Drake strode over to the window. "Erasmus!" he said. "Thank goodness! I wanted to have a word with him before he left. But what on earth can he mean by coming here so openly during daylight?"

Erasmus alighted on the lawn in front of the lodge, and Dr. Drake opened the window to greet him. A cold wind howled and the fire flared up.

The white dragon wasted no time. "You must come with me at once, Dragon Master. As for the rest of you, I must ask you to stay indoors. It will be for the best. There has been an unexpected development. I believe that we may be closer than we had thought to unravelling the mystery of my missing relatives."

✦ ✦ ✦

Dr. Drake had been gone for some time, and there was no telling when he might return. My parents retreated into the small sitting room that Father was using as an office while he drew up a plan of action to monitor the frost dragon situation. I, meanwhile, went to my room to write an account of the morning's tracking challenge in my dragonological record book. I was delighted when a rough scratching at my bedroom door heralded the arrival of Torcher. He went straight to the window and stood on his back legs, as he had done before, staring fixedly out at the sky.

"Is Erasmus out there again, old fellow?" I asked him, although I knew he could not understand more than a few basic words of English. "Or perhaps you can see some grouse and you are wondering what they would taste like."

Torcher ignored me, so I sat at the desk, opened my record book, and took up my pen from its resting place on the blotter. This was my third record book and it was nearing completion. Although we had made one or two mistakes in Erasmus's training exercise, I felt pleased that Beatrice and I had at least worked out that we were tracking a frost dragon. I turned to an earlier page, where I had painstakingly copied a picture of one, and wondered how on earth they could have disappeared so suddenly. Closing the book, I put down my pen, picked up my binoculars, and strolled across to join Torcher at the window. He seemed to be scanning the loch and the far hills nervously.

"What is it, Torcher?" I asked as I raised the binoculars to my eyes. "What can you see?"

Torcher made a funny noise in the back of his throat, as though he had something to say but didn't know how to say it. He snapped his jaws in frustration, then made a sudden lunge for the table and dragged my record book onto the floor. Holding it open with the end of his tail, he flicked through the pages with a razor-sharp claw.

"Be careful!" I shouted, failing hopelessly to recall the word for "careful" in Dragonish.

Torcher reached the picture of the frost dragon and touched it with the tip of his claw. I felt a sudden rush of excitement.

"Good boy!" I exclaimed. "But where is it? Where's the frost dragon, Torcher?"

This time when I held up my binoculars I could see it with perfect clarity. I gasped. It was a magnificent specimen, its white flanks tinged with just a hint of blue as it flashed across the sky like a silver comet.

CHAPTER THREE

THE CASTLE IN THE LOCH

Those who carp and prate that dragons —— even if they
existed —— would have mental abilities little greater than bonobos
or killer whales, are given the lie by the dragons' remarkable ability to
improvise savage attacks using whatever materials lie handiest.

—— *Dr. Ernest Drake, Letters to a Young Dragonologist*

I took the quickest route from my attic room to the
ground floor—sliding all the way down the polished
wooden banisters of the staircase—and found Beatrice in
the entrance hall with a puzzled frown on her face.

"You've seen it, too, haven't you?" she exclaimed.

I nodded excitedly. "Have you told Mother or Father?"

"I can't find them," she said. "Surely they wouldn't have
gone out without telling us?"

We shouted for them, but there was no reply. The hunting lodge was large and rambling, but not so big that they
would not be able to hear us. Meanwhile, Torcher, who had
scurried down the stairs with me, was clawing impatiently
at the latch on the front door.

"Perhaps they spotted the frost dragon and thought they'd better not risk any delays," I suggested.

Beatrice looked doubtful. "But Erasmus told us all to stay here," she said.

Suddenly there was a loud bang and a rush of cold wind. To my astonishment, Torcher had managed to open the front door and, before either of us could stop him, had dashed out. We had no choice but to follow him. Whatever the dangers, we had to keep Torcher hidden — most humans knew nothing of the existence of real, live dragons, and the S.A.S.D. wanted to keep things that way. In any case, after our recent run-in with Ignatius Crook, who had captured Torcher, I wasn't going to risk losing the little chick again.

We followed him to the road that snaked around the side of the loch. By the time we reached it, Torcher was already scampering across the causeway that led to a ruined castle.

"Torcher, wait!" I cried as he disappeared through an arched doorway. And then I saw something that filled my heart with terror. High above us, three black dragons were flying in circles: Tunguskas. War dragons. They were craning their necks as they searched for something on the ground. Beatrice had seen them, too, and her face turned white. If the Tunguskas had not spotted us before, they had most certainly seen us now, for they suddenly began diving towards us at tremendous speed. Beatrice took off, sprinting like a greyhound, and reached the castle entrance a few seconds before me. I felt a blast of air whip across my neck as the lead dragon swiped at me with an outstretched claw. I hurled myself through the doorway, leaving the dragon to roar in frustration.

It took me a few moments to get my breath back. Dr. Drake and Erasmus stood before us, staring at us in surprise. Next to them was the frost dragon that I had seen from my bedroom window. He had two long, ugly marks on his underbelly and inspected us with haughty, pale-grey eyes. I wondered if he had been in battle with the Tunguskas already.

"Is it safe—?" I began.

Dr. Drake held up his hand to silence me and glanced upwards. The ruined castle had no roof, and above us, the black dragons were circling in a patch of grey sky.

"They are too big to get in," said Erasmus. "We are safe for now. But we cannot stay here forever."

"At least if they have no way of attacking us it will give me time to think," said Dr. Drake. He turned to Beatrice and me. "What brings you here?"

"We were following Torcher," I gasped. "We couldn't find our parents in the lodge. We guessed that they must have seen the frost dragon, but didn't realise that you already knew about it."

"We have not seen your parents," said Erasmus. "I had only just seen the black dragons when I spoke to you. Then Dr. Drake and I discovered my brother, Tingi." The frost dragon inclined his head slightly. "Fortunately for you, he speaks English, although it may be rusty; he rarely converses with humans beyond the land of the frozen rivers." Erasmus turned to the superior-looking dragon. "Tingi, these are my human pupils, Daniel and Beatrice."

"*Praisich boyar!*" I exclaimed, bowing low. My sister did likewise.

"*Praisich hoyari,*" replied Tingi in a rumbling voice. "So you know some Dragonish?" he continued, in English. "That is well."

"You are the brother of Erasmus?" asked Beatrice.

"We are half brothers," put in Erasmus. "Tingi was just explaining what has happened to the rest of my kinsfolk."

"Alas!" cried Tingi, whose English did not seem rusty to me at all. "It is a tale of great sadness. Two moons past, I was hunting whales in the southern ocean, in order that I might feed before starting my journey to the north. But I was injured—"

I pointed to Tingi's underbelly. "Was that when you got those scars?"

Tingi nodded gravely. "I was hunting a humpback whale, but a pod of orcas disputed my prize and ambushed me as I dived into the ocean. Of course, they were no match for me and I feasted on orca instead; but I needed time to recover from my wounds, and when I returned home, my dragon kin had vanished."

"Where had they gone?" asked Beatrice, her face kind and concerned.

"At first I thought they had left on the journey north," Tingi explained. "But I soon realised that that was impossible. Their scent was mingled with the odour of another species of dragon, but not one I had ever encountered before. And there were traces of silver dragon dust that made me sleepy when I inhaled it."

"What did you do?" I asked.

"I had to fight the fatigue and carry on. Following the two scent trails, I discovered that a human female had used an army of black dragons to overpower my kinsfolk, enslaving them with a mixture of dragon dust and dark magic."

"Alexandra Gorynytchka!" breathed Beatrice.

"You know of her?" Tingi stared at Beatrice intently, then carried on with his story. "She took the other frost dragons to an island in the middle of the ocean, where she keeps them prisoner. I cannot discover why, for the island swarms with black dragons by day, and at night there is another terror: a gigantic, feathered amphithere that pursued me ruthlessly. I knew that I must seek help if my kinsfolk are to survive, so I came looking for my brother."

Beatrice glanced up at the sky. "And the Tunguskas followed you?" she asked. The menacing black creatures still wheeled above us.

"I thought I had shaken them off," replied Tingi, "but they must have followed my scent."

Beatrice wrinkled her brow. "So why didn't they just capture you? Why let just one frost dragon free?"

Dr. Drake turned to Tingi and asked sharply, "Did it not occur to you that you were being allowed to escape so that the Tunguskas could follow you?"

Tingi looked perplexed.

"Perhaps they guessed that you would fly to Erasmus," suggested Beatrice.

"But what could they possibly want with my brother?" said Tingi incredulously.

Dr. Drake's answer was drowned out by a sudden crashing noise overhead. A huge boulder was tumbling down. Beatrice launched herself at me, hurling me out of the way as it smashed to pieces on the ground where we had just been standing. But the danger was far from over. More boulders came hurtling into the ruin. Erasmus butted one away with his head, while another struck Torcher with a sickening thud. My heart jumped into my mouth, but before I had time to run to him, the dragon chick leapt up and roared furiously at the Tunguskas. The dark dragons seemed not to notice.

"I should have foreseen this!" cried Dr. Drake, wringing his hands anxiously. "They have found a way to attack us after all."

"Alexandra must know that we are here!" exclaimed Beatrice. "She has never forgiven us for finding that cure for the dragon plague. . . ."

Dr. Drake reached out to calm Beatrice. "I believe that Alexandra is after me," he said kindly. "That is why she allowed Tingi to fly to his brother. She knew that Erasmus would relay Tingi's story to me." He thought for a moment, then turned to the white dragon. "Erasmus, by the ancient pact between our two societies, I charge you to protect these children. Tingi, I beg you to assist him. Beatrice and Daniel must not come to any harm." He turned and headed for the door, stretching an arm out to indicate that we were to leave ahead of him. "The castle is doomed," he continued gravely. "We must flee."

As he strode onto the open causeway, another rock came crashing down, and Tingi moved swiftly to intercept it. Now there seemed to be Tunguskas everywhere.

"How many of them are there?" I cried as the archway above the door began to crack.

"I don't know," shouted Beatrice. "But we've got to get out!"

We ran through the doorway. Erasmus and Tingi were swooping towards us, but before they had a chance to rescue us, the black dragons blocked their way with a wall of red-and-yellow flame. Up on the hillside the hunting lodge was on fire. The roof was a blazing inferno; black smoke poured from the windows.

"Mother!" I cried. "Father!" I rushed forwards, but the exit from the causeway was barred by a Tunguska at the far end. There was no escape. I glanced at the icy loch, but Dr. Drake shook his head. Beatrice took hold of my hand and I looked at her wide-eyed. Was this the end?

Suddenly, with the tip of its wing almost whipping our

faces, the largest Tunguska dived down and plucked Dr. Drake from the causeway. I waited in horror for the spout of flame, or the bite to the head, that would finish him off, but neither came. Before I could move, another dragon grabbed Beatrice and dragged her away, screaming. All at once, I felt a razor-sharp claw circle my waist, now I, too, was captured. I was rigid with terror as my captor bore me into the sky with a triumphant roar. But at the last moment, Torcher leapt up and clamped his jaws around the dragon's leg.

The Tunguska tried to shake the smaller dragon off, but to no avail: the chick would not let go. It occurred to me at that moment that if my captor did not want to risk killing me in order to get rid of Torcher, then Alexandra must want us alive!

Torcher scrambled up alongside me, and I looked back just in time to see Tingi fall into the loch with an enormous splash; Erasmus was still fighting valiantly in the middle of a biting, clawing mob of black dragons. Tears filled my eyes. I was cold and frightened and I knew I could not survive a long journey, dangling from the dark creature's talons as I was. But after a few miles, the dragons turned towards a tall, flat-topped mountain. There, waiting for us, were three gigantic Tunguskas with mahout riders and wicker cages on their backs. By their side stood a man in a filthy black coat. I shuddered as we drew closer, for I knew the man only too well. He was Alexandra Gorynytchka's most coldhearted and ruthless agent, Shadwell. The moment we came in to land, Torcher leapt down and rushed at him. But Shadwell calmly flung his coat open to reveal a pistol, which he raised swiftly, aiming it directly at the young chick.

"Torcher, stop!" cried Beatrice, who, along with Dr. Drake, had landed before me.

"That's my girl," said Shadwell in his broad cockney accent, leering and keeping a firm hold on his gun.

"What have you done with our parents?" demanded Beatrice, bravely stepping in front of the dragon chick.

Shadwell raised his eyebrows in mock concern. "Oh, dear. Has something happened to them? Thank goodness the rest of you are unharmed."

"You are despicable," I said, raising my fist, but Dr. Drake restrained me.

"Release us, Shadwell," said Dr. Drake, "and I will pay you handsomely, if it is money you want."

"You know I cannot do that," the villain sneered.

"Then release Beatrice and Daniel," Dr. Drake suggested. "It is me that your mistress wants, is it not? She has no business to settle with the children."

Shadwell snapped his fingers. "Fiddlesticks!" he said, with an insincere grin. "My orders were to bring you and the two children. There was no mention of a dragon chick, though. So be good sports and climb up into those cages. I'll let Miss Gorynytchka decide what should be done with your young dragon friend. We've got a charming little ride ahead of us. They say it's going to be sunny."

Chapter Four

THE LOST ISLAND
OF DRAGONS

*To be suddenly cast into a danger so deadly that escaping with one's
life seems a laughable outcome is a situation to be eagerly
welcomed by those dragonologists who wish to try their mettle.*

—— *Dr. Ernest Drake, Letters to a Young Dragonologist*

We had been flying over the ocean for a whole day
when I spotted an island through the wicker bars
of my cage. It was not large, perhaps ten miles long by seven
broad, but in the middle, white smoke poured in a steady
column from a very active volcano. During the journey, the
mahout rider had twice crawled along the spiny neck of his
mount to our cage in order to bring food and water. He had
fed us, but otherwise Torcher and I had been left alone. I
had no idea of our location, except that the sun had risen on
my left and it was getting warmer; we were obviously flying
south.

At first, Torcher had struggled against the ropes that
bound him, but when he finally accepted that he could not

break free, he had slept for most of the journey, conserving his strength for coming conflict. I could not sleep, and I spent all my time brooding. I had to protect Beatrice and help Dr. Drake, not to mention finding out what had happened to my parents. And to accomplish those things, I needed to escape.

"Torcher," I called softly.

He opened his eyes.

"Show me your teeth," I said. At first he did not understand, but when I bared mine he realised what I meant. His jaws were bound, so he couldn't open them very wide, but it was enough. I rubbed the ropes that tied my hands against his sharp incisors and smiled in triumph as my bonds fell to the floor. Soon, both Torcher and I were untied and I quietly tried the door of the cage. To my relief it was unlocked.

"It's time to go," I said. I pointed to the sea. Our Tunguska was flying low over the ocean, but it still looked like a terrifying drop, and I had no idea whether there were jagged rocks or corals beneath the surface of the water. I hesitated. Dare I risk it? But then, the mahout driver made my mind up for me. He turned around, saw that Torcher and I were untied, and began shouting angrily.

"Go!" I cried to the dragon chick, closing my eyes as I leapt from the cage. It was the most frightening drop of my life, ending with a splash that knocked the air out of my lungs and sent me plunging deep under the surface in a whirl of bubbles. But I was still alive. I kicked as hard as I could and rose spluttering and gasping near the shore. Above me, I could see the black Tunguska flapping doggedly onwards — it was too large to manoeuvre quickly, and with that wicker contraption on its back there was no way it could attempt to pluck us from the sea. But now I had a different problem.

"Torcher!" I cried. "Torcher, where are you?" I began to panic. I could not see the dragon chick anywhere. Had he been too scared to jump? Perhaps he could not swim. I had not considered the possibility. An image of the brave little dragon's lifeless corpse sinking to the bottom of the ocean came to me, and I thrashed around, desperately trying to spot him. However, in doing so I attracted the attention of a party of Tunguskas who were flying out from the island. The current was carrying me towards some nearby rocks, and I prayed that I could reach them in time. I took a deep breath and dived under the water. It was too murky to see anything, and although I swam as fast as I could, it felt like an impossibly long way.

My lungs were bursting by the time I finally scraped a hand against some barnacles and came up for air. The dragons were nearer, but they were focussed on where I had been, rather than where I was now. I hid myself among the rocks, keeping my head just above the water and trying to stay still, though it was almost impossible in the swell. The dragons moved closer. How could I have been stupid enough to believe that they wouldn't find me? Suddenly, one of them spewed a jet of flame at something in the water, then picked up the object in its claws, only to drop it again in disgust — it was a piece of driftwood. I quickly pulled myself underwater and held my breath again as one of the dragons landed on the rocks next to me. Had it smelled me? It let out a deep growl and then, to my relief, took off and flew around in a wide circle. There was still no sign of Torcher.

It was at least an hour before the Tunguskas gave up searching for me and I was able to swim the short distance to the beach. I was exhausted, chilled to the bone, and my limbs ached from treading water, so I slumped on a rock and rested, knowing that the dragons might return at any moment. Black cliffs loomed behind the beach where I had come ashore. A sharp overhang of rock convinced me that climbing would be impossible. I looked farther along the beach and saw that the cliffs dropped straight into the sea, so I heaved myself up and set off in the opposite direction.

I made slow progress. Sodden clothes and my exhausted legs held me back. But after some forty minutes or so, I spotted dragon tracks that ran up from the shoreline and along the beach. They disappeared among the rocks at the foot of the cliffs. The tracks looked too small for a Tunguska; maybe Torcher could swim, after all. Suddenly I felt renewed hope. I wanted to shout out his name, but I daren't risk it for fear that the Tunguskas would hear. I consoled myself with the thought that if the tracks did belong to Torcher, then at least we were both travelling in the same direction. With any luck, I would find him waiting for me up ahead.

I set off energetically now, but had not gone far before I realised that the tide was rising and the strip of beach was shrinking fast. Soon, the sea would be washing over my shoes. I had to get to higher ground. As I clambered over boulders towards the cliffs, I was almost knocked backwards by one of the strangest, most pungent odours I have ever experienced in my life. Closer to the cliffs, the smell grew even more intense, and I could just make out the dark mouth of a cave hidden in a cleft a few feet above the white mark of the waterline.

By now the waves were lapping around my ankles, and I had no choice but to scramble up to the cave. But my relief on reaching the cave soon turned to horror, for the entrance was piled high with bones and skulls—each and every one of which was human! I gritted my teeth, trying to ignore them, and, pulling my collar over my nose as protection from the stench, I picked my way deeper into the cave. It was hard to see in the gloom, but something inside was definitely moving. I stood stock-still, my heart thumping wildly, and let my eyes adjust to the darkness.

At last I spotted something, and my heart nearly burst with relief, for sitting in the corner of the cave, twisting his head happily this way and that, was Torcher! I wanted to cry out, but it was just as well I stopped myself, for at that moment I spotted something else, and the returning sense of horror brought on goose bumps the length of my body. As my vision grew clearer, I was able to pick out a vast, living shape that virtually covered the floor of the cave. The enormous creature had a coiled, snakelike body and a huge, plumed head. Its great wings were loosely folded over a glistening pile of gold and silver trinkets, held in place within the coils of the spine as it rose and fell rhythmically. By its plumes, I judged this to be a male amphithere. And by some uncharacteristic good fortune, I realised that he was asleep!

But had Torcher even noticed the giant beside him? From the way the little dragon acted, blinking innocently in the darkness, I assumed he had not.

"Torcher!" I whispered as loudly as I dared.

The chick stood up and looked about him.

"Torcher, over here!"

He spotted me and, to my relief, did not let out a roar of greeting, but padded over quietly and stood among the piled-up skeletons looking down at me.

"Come here!" I said. I held out my arms to him, but his gaze shifted to the sea, and he looked doubtful.

"You can do it, Torcher. You can swim!"

Torcher was not convinced. Instead, he leaned forwards, clamped his jaws around the sleeve of my jacket, and pulled hard, tugging me back into the cave.

"No, Torcher, you have to come down!"

I tried to shake my arm free, but he had grown very strong.

"Let go, Torcher!" I pointed to the bones with my free hand and then at the sleeping dragon. "Dragon not good," I hissed, wagging my finger back and forth. "He eats people." But Torcher would not give way. On the far side of the sleeping amphithere there was a dim beam of natural light. Was Torcher trying to show me another way out? The young dragon scampered ahead of me and off into the distance.

Full of misgivings, I tiptoed after him towards the rear of the cave. There was only the narrowest of gaps between the sleeping amphithere and the cave wall, and as I reached the dragon, his breath was hot on my face. I had almost grown used to the stench, but suddenly the great dragon began to snore so loudly that I was forced to press both hands over my ears. I turned sideways to slip past the vast creature and beheld the entrance to a stairway that disappeared upwards into the rock. My heart leapt! It was too small for the amphithere to follow me, even if he had been awake. I took one step, then another, but something was blocking the way — a gigantic feathery tail that seemed at once soft and scaly. I looked back in a panic. Two green eyes contemplated me with fury. The amphithere, wide awake now, began babbling in a host of different languages. Then, loud and all too clear, I heard the English words, "Stay and declare your business, stranger, or I will tear you limb from limb!"

CHAPTER FIVE

KOA

Make them laugh, make them cry, but make them talk:
words of wisdom for those foolish enough to awaken
a sleeping dragon in its den.

—— *Dr. Ernest Drake, Letters to a Young Dragonologist*

O nly those who have been cornered by a dragon can
ever understand what it really feels like to be faced
with powerful muscles rippling along coils that can crush
without mercy; to hear the snap of teeth that can crack
bones to splinters; to smell searing breath that can turn flesh
to charred meat. I was paralysed with fear; it was impossible
to think. Only the sight of Torcher squirming through the
feathers of the creature's tail steeled my nerves. I shook
myself. I had to find Beatrice and Dr. Drake. I had to stay
alive!

"*Praisich boyar!*" I exclaimed, using the traditional
Dragonish greeting and bowing low. The amphithere's eyes
widened, then narrowed to slits. A warning rumble came
from his throat.

"The fact that you speak Dragonish neither excuses you, nor marks you as a friend," he said. "How dare you enter my lair unbidden?"

"I am a friend to dragons," I said. "My name is Daniel. I come in peace."

"A friend to dragons? Why should I believe you?"

"I was escaping the rising tide — and following my companion. I should have sought your permission to enter, and for that, I apologise. However, if it will satisfy you, I offer you a riddle challenge."

"Why? I have neither treasure nor wisdom to offer in return."

I glanced at the grisly trophies by the entrance to the cave. "For my life. And for that of my companion."

The amphithere looked at Torcher with new interest. "By 'companion,' you mean this dragon chick?"

"I do. His name is Torcher."

"Torcher is in no danger from me. But a human, on the other hand, trying to sneak into my lair while I am asleep . . ." The dragon paused before continuing. "My name is Koa and I am the last of a lost race. I have little love for humans and no interest in your riddles. You are not the first human to try to enter my lair uninvited."

I shuddered as I looked once more at the bones strewn about the floor. Were they all that remained of other unfortunate dragonologists? I looked at them more carefully now, and I noticed something new: they were not adult size. Did this dragon eat children? Clutching my hand to my chest, I cursed the terrible mistake I had made in entering the cave. But then my hand rested on the cold metal of the dragon whistle that hung about my neck, and I had an idea that I hoped might save me. In Britain my dragon whistle could summon any one of a number of dragons to my aid, but on this island I did not know what — if any — assistance it would bring. But it was my only hope.

"Take this," I said, holding out the whistle. "It is all the treasure I have. Take it and let me go."

Koa's breath was hot and pungent on my face as he leaned forwards to inspect the whistle. But if he recognised it, or was impressed by it, he did not show it.

"It is a pretty toy, but do you really believe that I would exchange your life for a trinket such as this?"

Suddenly, in spite of my terror, I felt consumed by anger. "I do not think you understand," I said. "This is not a toy. It is a dragon whistle, given to me by the Master of Hong Wei Temple, in China. It is the most precious thing that I own."

The great dragon threw back his crested head. "Pah, if I wanted your dragon whistle I could simply keep it after I have killed you!" He made a rumbling noise in his throat. It was a grim and menacing sound, but I stood my ground. "You are courageous, at least," he continued. "Most humans would fall to their knees and weep with terror at the mere sight of me."

I looked Koa squarely in the face. "I told you: I am a

friend to dragons. If you let me go, I promise that you shall never see me again. But if you — decide — well, not to let me go — please, make the end quick. And, I beg you, help this dragon chick."

"Very well, I shall let you go." Koa sighed and was thoughtful for a moment. "But you must leave this island immediately. If you return you will forfeit your life."

With that, Koa lifted his tail so that the tunnel was no longer blocked, and I moved swiftly past, to safety.

The dim light grew brighter as Torcher and I climbed the stone stairway and hastened along a narrow tunnel full of fantastical carvings of amphitheres and of men and women wearing strange, conical hats and long, brocaded gowns. I wondered what sort of people they had been, for these images suggested that they had lived peacefully alongside dragons — how I wished we could live like that today. I spotted a sliver of daylight up ahead, and my steps quickened in my eagerness to escape the darkness. But before I had made much progress at all, the floor of the tunnel shook violently and I was flung to the ground. A series of violent explosions thundered deep within the earth. They were answered by an angry roar from Koa, down below. Had I escaped the amphithere only to die in an earthquake? The rocks around me began to crumble, and I crawled, scrabbling across the rubble on bleeding hands and knees, as more and more pieces of stone thundered around me, each threatening to crush or impale me. I cried out and covered my head with my hands, convinced that the end had come. But the explosions ceased as suddenly as they had started, and the tunnel became still once more. I crawled on, breathless and shaking, and reached the exit at last. Pulling myself out, wearily, I blinked in the sudden daylight and took in my new surroundings. I had left the tunnel through a hole in the cliffs, roughly one hundred feet above sea level. At first, Torcher was nowhere to be seen. I worried that he had dived down into the ocean. Then I heard a familiar roar and looked up: he was a few feet above me, clinging to the cliff wall. I spotted tiny hand- and footholds carved into the rock face and started to climb up after him.

Now I was completely exposed: not only would another earthquake dislodge me and throw me to my death on the rocks below, but any passing dragon could spot me with ease. I looked over my shoulder and saw a party of Tunguskas flying towards the island from some distance away. They seemed not to have noticed me, but it could only be a matter of time. I climbed quickly until I reached the point where Torcher was waiting for me.

"Good dragon!" I said. "That was a near thing, eh, boy?"

Now I needed to decide on my next move. I guessed that the best thing to do was to head inland and put as much distance between myself and Koa as possible. The pillar of smoke rising from the volcano had grown thicker, and I could see dragons circling the peak. There was no evidence of human habitation, so I could not guess where Dr. Drake and Beatrice might be. I looked for Torcher, and I saw he was exploring a little ahead of me. He seemed untroubled, and I was smiling at his curious explorations, when he suddenly went rigid, his back arching like an angry cat's.

As I drew closer I became aware of distant noises: loud bangs and cries. Could those be human voices I heard, too? Then came a louder rumbling; it sounded as though the cliff itself were beginning to crumble — like the earthquake we had felt in the cave. There was a steep slope in front of us, and the sound seemed to be coming from the other side. With Torcher sticking close by me now, I scrambled up the slope until I crested the ridge.

Even in my wildest dreams I could not have imagined the sight that met me. Before us lay an enormous pit full of Tunguskas and frost dragons, all of them held by huge chains. Thousands of men swarmed among them, shovelling stone into carts. I watched as one Tunguska stepped up to a rock face on the side of the pit and spat out a jet of flame. A frost dragon stepped up after him and emitted an icy blast in the exact same spot, and eventually, the rock shattered and tumbled to the ground. So this is what had become of the frost dragons! Alexandra had enslaved them to work for her. But what sort of work was this? I shuddered to think what terrible prize could be worth the freedom of so many dragons. At that moment, Torcher let out a stifled roar. I turned to hush him and, as I did, caught sight of an all-too-familiar shape disappearing among the rocks.

"Flitz!" I hissed. Alexandra Gorynytchka's pet dwarf dragon, Flitz, was a wicked creature, and the instant I saw him, I knew that my presence would be reported. I turned to flee, but it was too late! A party of uniformed men were already upon us. One of the men, who seemed to be in charge, rushed forwards and grabbed my hair, jerking my head backwards and holding me there. Another threw a net over Torcher's head. The little dragon struggled, but to no avail.

"Open your mouth," the first man demanded. He spoke with what I guessed was a Russian accent.

I shook with fear as he held up a small, uncapped bottle.

"Open it!" he repeated fiercely, an angry frown forming on his brow.

I kept my mouth firmly shut, but one of his leering companions leaned over me and closed my nostrils with greasy fingers, forcing his dirty thumb into the side of my mouth so that I had to open it. I gagged and tried to shake my head.

"You want to escape, yes?" said the man with the bottle. "Try to escape now!" And with that he laughed coldly and poured the bitter liquid down my throat. I had no choice but to swallow the drug. My knees buckled under me and soon the whole world went dark.

CHAPTER SIX

DISASTER

The field dragonologist who makes it his business to study
the deadliest species will soon become used to a sense of
very real impending doom.

—— *Dr. Ernest Drake, Letters to a Young Dragonologist*

I awoke with a start from my drugged slumber and discovered I was in a cave. Words can hardly describe my surprise and delight at finding Beatrice and Dr. Drake both leaning over me, their faces full of concern. Beatrice's eyes were moist and red. I wondered what dreadful adventure she had been through before arriving here.

"Where are we, Bea?" I said. "Are you both all right?"

"Yes, yes, Daniel, and thank goodness you're safe," said Beatrice, clutching my hand. "They told us that you'd drowned. We don't know what they are planning to do with us, but we're safe, so far. Where's Torcher? And what happened to you?"

"Didn't they bring Torcher here?"

"No," said Dr. Drake. "When they carried you in, you were mumbling in your sleep about Torcher and someone called Koa."

"They drugged me," I explained. "How long have I been asleep?"

"You have been with us for nearly a day," Dr. Drake answered.

"A day!" I leapt to my feet.

"Daniel, calm down. What's wrong?" asked Beatrice.

"I tried to escape. I dived into the sea with Torcher, and"—I looked around wildly—"I know what has happened to the frost dragons."

As I recounted my adventures to Beatrice and Dr. Drake, their eyes grew ever wider. I explained how Koa had ordered me to leave the island and how Torcher and I had been captured.

"Poor Torcher!" exclaimed Beatrice.

But Dr. Drake smiled. "Do not fear too much for Torcher," he said. "That little dragon is braver and cleverer than he looks."

Beatrice seemed puzzled. "There's one thing I don't understand. If Alexandra keeps all of these dragons as slaves, then why does she let one dragon roam free on the island?"

"Perhaps Koa is an ally," I suggested.

"Yes, but then he would have handed you over, wouldn't

he? And why is she getting the dragons to break up the rocks in the first place?"

"She's obviously searching for something," said Dr. Drake.

"Well, it must be something important if she's going to all that trouble."

Dr. Drake frowned. "I believe that Miss Gorynytchka needs our help. Otherwise, why would she have brought us here?"

"Our help?" Beatrice sounded sceptical.

"Yes. It is clear to me where we are now. Alexandra must have found the fabled Lost Island of Dragons."

"You mean the place where Ignatius Crook found the basilisk wand?" Now my sister looked fearful.

Dr. Drake nodded and tugged at his moustache. "There is a tale in *Liber Draconis*—dismissed as a legend by most members of the S.A.S.D.—that this island once formed a part of the lost continent of Atlantis. Of course, you should know from your schoolbooks that Atlantis was drowned under the sea after a terrible catastrophe. But what you will not find in your books is that according to *Liber Draconis,* a single island survived, populated by a remarkable race of amphitheres."

"What was remarkable about them?" I asked.

"They had a number of unusual traits. They were very friendly with humans, for a start, and they lived in a dragon city built at the foot of a volcano."

"A dragon city!" Beatrice was incredulous, but it was obvious from Dr. Drake's expression that he was deadly earnest.

"Then that must be what she is searching for!" I exclaimed, remembering the carvings in the tunnel leading from Koa's lair. "But if this is where the basilisk wand was discovered, does that mean there are basilisks here?"

Dr. Drake frowned. "Not necessarily, Daniel. The wand may have been left here by visitors to the island. The Vikings are almost certain to have spent time here, and even Beatrice Croke is said to have visited."

"Beatrice Croke? The founder of the S.A.S.D.? What was she doing here?"

Dr. Drake's hand went to his waistcoat pocket and he drew out a large gem on the end of a thick, golden chain. Inside the jewel floated an ethereal image of his own face. It was the Dragon's Eye gem, which marked him out as Dragon Master. "I fear that the dragon city is not Alexandra's chief goal on the island. It is time that I told you something," he said.

"About the Dragon's Eye?" asked Beatrice.

"Not directly," Dr. Drake replied. "But it does concern the treasures of the Secret and Ancient Society of Dragonologists, of which the Dragon's Eye is an important part." He paused, to ensure he held our attention. "When Ebenezer Crook sent me the clue that helped us to find this gem — the clue to the gravestone riddle in Bodmin that Beatrice was clever enough to unravel—he sent me another message on a piece of dragon skin that faded even as I read it."

"What did it say?" asked Beatrice.

"It said: 'Beware the thirteenth treasure.'"

"The thirteenth treasure! But I thought there were only twelve treasures," I said.

Before Dr. Drake had a chance to answer, two armed men burst into the cave, followed by Shadwell.

"So you have woken up at last, Daniel? Then it's time for a stroll in the fresh air." He smirked. Shadwell nodded to the men, and one of them produced a set of keys and unlocked our cell.

"It won't be fresh for long if you're in it," mumbled Beatrice, just loud enough for Shadwell to hear. He pulled the pistol from inside his coat and pointed it at me.

"I'm going to ask you to do me the favour of shutting your mouth, missy. And as for you, Daniel, Miss Gorynytchka says that she has been very lenient with you up to now. But she won't tolerate any further attempts to escape. All right?"

"Are you taking us to see her?" asked Dr. Drake.

"I'm taking the children to see her. You are to wait here until further orders."

Dr. Drake blanched. "But the children cannot help her. I am the only one who can assist her."

Shadwell shrugged, then used his pistol to wave Beatrice and me through the iron doorway. I took hold of my sister's hand and squeezed it. I knew that she was thinking the same thing as me: how could we face Alexandra Gorynytchka without Dr. Drake?

Outside I had to shade my eyes against the bright sunlight. There was no possibility of escape, for we were high up on a ridge that ran to the summit of the volcano, and on either side of us were sheer drops. Two Tunguska dragons were perched on a nearby crag, and they shadowed us silently as we proceeded along the precipitous path. I looked down fearfully and, as I did so, caught sight of something moving stealthily behind a rocky outcrop, apparently keeping up with us.

"Flitz!" I spat out the name, but no one heard me. Suddenly the entire island started to shake as three sharp blasts exploded deep within the volcano. Shadwell stumbled behind me, his yellow grin fading into an alarmed gasp. I realised with a sick lurch that the earthquake might very easily cause his finger to slip on the trigger of the pistol that he kept trained on me. Below us, rocks became dislodged by the earthquake and tumbled towards the jungle. *If only one of them would dislodge Flitz,* I thought. Then, as suddenly as it had started, the earthquake ceased and a sinister calm descended on the island once more.

My eyes watered and my throat itched unbearably as we approached the top of the volcano. The sulphurous gases were growing ever thicker and more acrid. About a hundred yards from the summit, Shadwell stopped and waved his pistol.

"You can go on alone from here. She's waiting for you."

Only the two Tunguskas followed us now, and up ahead, I could see Alexandra Gorynytchka pacing back and forth near the rim of the crater. She seemed unaffected by the fumes. Her red lips twisted into a hideous mockery of a kindly smile when she saw us, and I squeezed Beatrice's hand all the harder.

"Daniel and Beatrice! How delightful to see you." The odious woman held out her arms, and my gaze darted back to the Tunguskas, who were blocking the only route off the summit. I remembered just how much I hated her.

"We can't say the same about you," hissed Beatrice. "We thought that you were dead."

For a moment Alexandra's face contorted in a spasm of rage, but then she regained her composure and let out a sneering laugh. "I am terribly sorry to disappoint you."

"What have you done with our parents?" I demanded.

"Ah, yes, your poor, long-suffering parents. Whatever can have happened to them?" Alexandra pushed out her bottom lip, feigning an unhappy pout. "My orders were for them to be brought here alive or dead, but they couldn't be found in either condition. I must say, though, I was surprised that the Tunguskas who brought you here were not a good deal hungrier after their tiring ride. Perhaps they stopped off for a dragonological feast in Scotland.

Would that explain it?" She obviously was not going to answer my first question honestly, but I could not resist trying another.

"Why have you made slaves of the frost dragons?" I demanded.

Alexandra laughed again. "Oh, you've seen them, Daniel, haven't you? Fire and ice make such pretty companions, don't you agree?"

Beatrice gave Alexandra a cool look. "You're inhuman."

Alexandra clamped her bony hand on my shoulder and then did the same to Beatrice, grasping us both tightly. "Come with me," she said. "I want to show you something." She pushed us towards the rim of the crater. White smoke was rising from the far end of the pit, where the orange lava was brightest. I felt my face reddening in the heat and my chest tighten against the choking gases.

Still holding us firmly in her grip, Alexandra leaned forwards into the sulphur cloud, her eyes wide and shining. She inhaled deeply, unaffected by the stench. "Can you smell that?" she breathed. "It is the scent of power! The true power of the earth that gave birth to dragons and all other creatures. My men don't like to come here; they fear the gases will drive them to madness, but to me this smell is a sweet balm!" Beatrice and I exchanged horrified glances. Alexandra had always been driven by a dark will; she had always craved power, but now she sounded recklessly unhinged, as though she were capable of any kind of

madness. "Behold!" she cried, spreading her arms wide. "A volcano gave birth to this island, and a volcano will destroy it! The earthquakes you have felt are just the beginning. This place is doomed. Our time here is short! We might still have a few weeks, or it could be merely days."

"What?" said Beatrice, startled. Her exclamation seemed to break whatever spell held Alexandra in its thrall, for when she spoke again, her voice was deep and calm.

"That is why I need friends such as you," she said. "We shall make a deal. You are Dr. Drake's star pupils. You were the ones who helped to discover the Dragon's Eye and caused the destruction of the Grand Lodge of Dragonsbane; you revealed the secrets of *Liber Draconis* and discovered the cure for the dragon plague—"

I could bear the tension no longer. "What do you want?" I snapped.

"I want to know what Dr. Drake taught you about this island, and about one thing in particular: an ancient weapon that was stolen long, long ago. Some call it the thirteenth treasure of the Secret and Ancient Society of Dragonologists; others, the most efficient weapon ever to be wielded by the Dragonsbane Knights."

"I don't know what you are talking about," I said.

Alexandra leaned over me, forcing me farther back towards the crater's edge. "Oh, but I see from your face that you do know, Daniel," she said. "It is called the Hammer of the Dragons, and it is hidden in a secret cavern on this island."

Beatrice let out a bitter laugh. "And I suppose you think that we are going to help you to find it?"

Alexandra pushed Beatrice back beside me; the slightest shove now and either one of us could fall to our death. "You know the secret of how to open that cavern, don't you? Dr. Drake has told you."

"No, we don't." I felt the waves of volcanic heat searing my back. I closed my eyes; they watered from the sting of the sulphurous steam.

"You are a liar, Daniel Cook. Open your eyes and look at me! If you help me, I will help you. If you thwart me, on the other hand, then you shall be made to suffer."

Somehow, the hopelessness of our situation made me feel wantonly courageous. I laughed. "What are you going to do?" I said. "You can't make me know something I don't know, even if you kill me."

Alexandra laughed and relaxed her grip on me ever so slightly. "You are a brave but very stupid boy, Daniel Cook. I wasn't thinking of harming you. But it wouldn't take much to push Beatrice over the edge, now, would it?"

I was aghast.

"But why do you need the Hammer of the Dragons?" cried Beatrice. "What does it do? Do you need to control even more dragons? Isn't your army complete?"

"To control them?" Alexandra laughed and glanced at the two Tunguskas who could clearly hear nothing of what she was saying. "Are you pretending that you don't know what the hammer does? How it destroys them?"

"I don't know. And Daniel doesn't either—do you, Daniel?" said Beatrice. "And Dr. Drake will never tell you anything."

"Perhaps. And perhaps not." Without releasing Beatrice, Alexandra grasped the back of my neck and pulled my ear close to her mouth. "You tell me, Daniel," she whispered. "Or Beatrice dies."

"No," I said. "I don't know anything. Please."

"No?" said Alexandra. "You dare refuse me?" Her eyes flashed and I could see the madness rising up in her again. "Then let us see if Dr. Drake is willing to be so cavalier about your sister's fate."

Alexandra whistled and the Tunguskas parted. A few moments later, Shadwell pushed Dr. Drake forwards. They had been behind us all the while, and by the haggard look on Dr. Drake's face, I could tell that he had seen everything, just as Alexandra had intended.

As Dr. Drake passed the Tunguskas, he gave them a sidelong glance.

"Do not even think about trying any of your dragonological charms on those two," cried Alexandra. "They are not hypnotised. I raised them myself, and they place my personal safety above all other considerations."

"Miss Gorynytchka," said Dr. Drake as calmly as he could manage. "I must say that we have met under pleasanter circumstances."

"The time for pleasantries between us ended long ago, Drake," she said. "You will reveal to me at once how to enter the cavern where the Hammer of the Dragons is kept, or these children will be thrown alive into the volcano."

For a fleeting moment, Dr. Drake stared at Alexandra in horror, as though he, too, had only now become aware of the full depth of the insanity lurking beneath the surface of her rational mind. But he quickly recovered his composure. "Miss Gorynytchka," he said. "I can certainly try to find out the location of the Hammer of the Dragons with you, but . . ."

"No buts, Drake. Perhaps you have mistaken me for someone with whom you can reason." She clicked her fingers and the Tunguskas lumbered towards us.

Dr. Drake looked ashen. "Please do not hurt Beatrice and Daniel," he said. "Do as you wish with me. I do not have any idea where the cavern that holds the Hammer of the Dragons is, far less how it may be opened. But I will help you."

"You are lying, Drake. You already know where it is. Dragon, throw the girl into the crater. *Hoyara algrai tyfur!*"

I watched in horror as a Tunguska curled its tail around Beatrice's waist and lifted her up so that her feet dangled over the fiery pit. She kicked and screamed.

"No!" I begged. "Please."

"Well, Doctor?" Alexandra folded her arms. "Are you going to let her die?"

"How can I save her when I do not know the information you seek?" Dr. Drake sounded broken. "All I can offer you is *Liber Draconis*. But, please, Beatrice is innocent in all of this. Don't hurt her."

As Dr. Drake and I watched, horror-struck, Beatrice's protestations slowed, until she hung from the Tunguska's tail like a limp doll, overwhelmed by the volcano's fumes. I felt helpless and desperate. There was a long pause in which Alexandra looked from Dr. Drake to Beatrice and back again. At last she broke the silence. "How do I read *Liber Draconis*? That idiot Ignatius Crook once said something about needing four dragons."

"You do need four dragons. But, please, put Beatrice down. Then I will explain everything.

"Tell me everything now."

"But she will die!"

"Then you had better be quick, or the boy will follow her."

I had no doubt that Alexandra would carry out her threat, and I could think of no way to save my sister or myself. Seeing movement near some rocks at the edge of the crater, I gloomily surmised it must be Flitz. But it wasn't the dwarf dragon at all. To my utter amazement, it was Torcher. Somehow he had managed to escape and follow us! With an angry roar, he leapt from his hiding place and looped his tail around one of the Tunguska's powerful legs. The distraction gave me a moment to take action.

I flung myself at Miss Gorynytchka, a whirlwind of fists and fury. "Leave my sister alone! Let her go," I hollered.

"Don't be a fool, Daniel," cried Dr. Drake. He moved as if to help me, but Shadwell grabbed him and held him back. I turned and gaped in horror as the Tunguska casually relaxed its grip on Beatrice, and she began to fall into the simmering volcano. There was nothing I or any other human could do. But there was still a small chance that a dragon could save her. Out of the corner of my eye, I saw Torcher swing into action. He leaned out over the ledge and grabbed the collar of Beatrice's jacket between his jaws, then valiantly dragged my sister back to safety before the lumbering black dragon had realised what was happening.

But it was not over yet. Alexandra lunged towards me and overpowered me in a moment. She twisted my arm behind my back, clamped her hand over my mouth, and dragged me to the crater's edge.

"Let Daniel go!" roared Dr. Drake, still struggling in Shadwell's grip. Alexandra glanced towards him and I sank my teeth into her hand; she let out a satisfying shriek of pain, but it was not enough to stop her.

At last Dr. Drake managed to wrestle himself free of Shadwell, and he dodged past the Tunguskas that were lumbering towards us. He pulled me from Alexandra's grasp, but soon he and Alexandra were locked in a deadly embrace, teetering on the edge of the precipice.

For an instant, his eye caught mine. "Get away from here!" he cried breathlessly. "Take Beatrice and Torcher."

"We're not leaving without you," I said.

"You must!" he gasped. "Someone has to get the word out. Go!"

One of the Tunguskas lunged out at Dr. Drake, separating him from Alexandra. Now both dragons rounded on him; Alexandra had turned white with rage.

"No!" she screamed. "Do not hurt him! I need him!"

But to my amazement the dragons ignored her. It seemed that once their dragon fury had reached its zenith, they could not be controlled, even by Alexandra. With heads down, they ran at Dr. Drake like a pair of enraged bulls, butting him over the edge of the crater towards the bubbling lava beyond. It took only a few seconds, and the Dragon Master was gone.

CHAPTER SEVEN

ESCAPE

*It was not long before I learned that if you are a friend
to dragons, you will make enemies.*

—— *Dr. Ernest Drake, Letters to a Young Dragonologist*

For a few moments after Dr. Drake had disappeared into the volcano, I sank to my knees, overwhelmed by the shock of what I had just seen. Somewhere in the distance, I became aware of a strange howling noise, like a fell wind. It was Alexandra, shrieking with uncontrollable rage as she pummelled the Tunguskas with her fists.

"You stupid brutes!" she shouted. "You will destroy everything! Find him. Bring him back to me alive! He must tell me what he knows."

Beatrice had crouched down at the edge of the crater and was leaning out over it, repeatedly calling Dr. Drake's name. I was devastated: my world had collapsed around me. I wanted to fling myself at Alexandra and push her into the fiery pit, too, the devil with the consequences. I scrambled over to the rim of the crater, but could see no sign of Dr. Drake. He must have been swallowed up and incinerated instantly. I could hardly bear to think of it.

Feeling someone — or something — tugging at my leg, I quickly regained my senses. Looking down, I found that Torcher had taken hold of my trouser leg between his teeth, in order to attract my attention. Up ahead, Shadwell's men had heard the commotion and finally decided to risk the gases around the rim of the crater. I could see them coming to Alexandra's assistance.

"Beatrice," I said. "We have to get out of here."

My sister looked up, her eyes wet with tears.

"We have to go," I said urgently.

But now the men were blocking the only route off the summit, and Shadwell was deep in conversation with Alexandra.

"Go?" Beatrice looked blank. "Where?"

"I think Torcher has an idea. Don't you, Torcher?"

The dragon chick trotted away from us to a narrow strip of rock that lay between the crater on one side and a steep slope on the other. A poisonous mist of white steam lingered among the rocks, making it hard to breathe. I laughed in disbelief.

"You want us to jump into the volcano, Torcher?" I exclaimed, incredulous, pointing over the edge of the crater to make sure that I had interpreted his meaning correctly. "You think we can find Dr. Drake?"

But Torcher turned to face the other way.

"You want us to jump down that cliff?" I pointed again, to be certain.

"*Sssssorrr,*" he said, using the Dragonish word for "yes." "*Sssssorrr.*" He was deadly earnest.

I nodded. "All right, Torcher," I said. It was literally a leap of faith, but in that instant I felt I owed it to the memory of Dr. Drake to believe that Torcher was braver and cleverer than he seemed. I had to believe that the dragon chick could help us. I turned to Beatrice. We had only a few precious seconds, and I could see that Shadwell, though still in discussion with Alexandra, had already drawn his pistol.

"Let's follow Torcher!" I hissed, trying to cough back the burning steam that was filling my lungs.

Beatrice struggled to her feet. A moment later she was at my side, looking at Torcher with incomprehension.

"I can hardly breathe here, and my eyes are stinging. Where does he want us to go?"

Torcher ran to the edge of the steep slope. Beatrice laughed bitterly as tears streamed down her face. "He thinks we can fly, don't you, Torcher? But we can't fly, Torcher. We can't. And neither can you."

Shadwell was advancing, his pistol trained on us. I prayed that the suffocating steam would put him off following us.

"Come back out of there," he ordered, from the edge of the cloud. "Don't make any sudden moves."

I edged towards the dragon chick. "Torcher knows we can't fly," I said to Beatrice. "We have to follow him. He knows what he's doing."

Beatrice's eyes were wide with terror. It was clear that the steep slope ended in a vertical drop, but there was no way of telling how long that drop was.

"I can't," she said. "I just can't."

"We have to," I said. "There's no way back, and Alexandra has to be stopped. We must get word to the S.A.S.D."

Beatrice nodded, stepped up to the edge, and closed her eyes. "For Dr. Drake, then," she said, her voice firm with resolution.

"For Dr. Drake," I said.

And we both jumped.

We fell for what seemed an eternity, tumbling so that the sky and earth and distant sea were nothing more than a whirl of blurred images. I caught glimpses of Beatrice falling above me, and I guessed that Torcher was somewhere beyond her. I prayed that he knew what he was doing, and I tried not to imagine the consequences if he did not. The drop was long and sickening; we seemed to move in slow motion. As I clipped a rocky outcrop with a painful thud, I grew more certain that I was about to meet my end; I saw nothing below me to break my fall. Then, all at once, I

landed with a splash in a deep jungle pool at the bottom of a towering waterfall.

Worrying now about piranhas and deadly water snakes, I thrashed my way to the bank, and just as I did so, Beatrice plunged into the water beside me. I looked up at the waterfall and, in disbelief, back at the near-vertical cliff that we had just tumbled down. No one pursued us — yet — but we could not stay in this place for more than a few moments. We had landed at the head of a narrow gorge. My eyes followed a stream that ran from the pool down the hillside.

"Where's Torcher?" Beatrice had stumbled from the water, her voice quivering.

"I don't know," I said, shielding my eyes from the bright sunlight and scanning the ground for tracks.

"Well, we can't wait here — look!" Beatrice gestured at a Tunguska wheeling far above us.

"Come on," I said. "If Torcher found us before, then he can find us again."

Not daring to waste a second, we set off down the narrow gorge, but its jungle foliage became so dense that we were forced to wade through the stream in order to make progress. When it seemed safe, we sat and rested in a shady spot. We had to make a plan.

Beatrice looked grim but determined. "I know what you are thinking, Daniel, and I'm thinking it, too. We have to get a message to Idraigir and the S.A.S.D., and we absolutely have to find a way of stopping Alexandra from getting her hands on the Hammer of the Dragons. But how?"

"Well, as far as we know, this island isn't marked on ordinary maps, so I doubt if there will be any passing boats. Probably all of Alexandra's men arrived by dragon. The island is not very large. The skies are swarming with Tunguskas. And then there is—"

"Koa," said Beatrice.

My heart sank. For a brief moment I had fooled myself that we had a chance. "It really is hopeless, isn't it?"

"We mustn't give up." Beatrice stood up and pointed down the gorge. There was a gap in the trees, and the distant sea was just visible beyond a rocky plain. I could see a tall stone standing on its own on a promontory. "That looks man-made," she said. "And didn't Dr. Drake say that the thirteenth treasure had something to do with human visitors to the island? Why don't we investigate that?"

"Perhaps. But look over there," I said, indicating a wisp of smoke rising up from the plain. "That looks like the pit where the dragons are working. We know from Tingi that Alexandra is using dragon dust to control them, so there must be a supply of dust somewhere. Maybe we could use some to free one of the frost dragons, then it could fly us off the island to raise the alarm."

Beatrice looked doubtful.

"What about the guards?" she said. "And what about

the Tunguskas? And don't forget, Flitz is down there somewhere."

"All right, then," I said, rising to my feet, ready for action. "Let's go and investigate the standing stone first. We need to learn everything we can about this island if we are to stand any chance of keeping Alexandra away from that hammer."

The climb down out of the gorge was slow and tedious, and the wide skirt of land that ran down to the sea seemed endless. Despite our anguish over Dr. Drake, we began to feel pangs of hunger, for we had not eaten for quite some time, so when Torcher caught up with us, some two hours later, not only were we overjoyed to see him, but we were grateful, too. He was carrying a small rucksack in his mouth that contained simple provisions—ship's biscuit and hard cheese—which he must have filched from Alexandra's men.

"Good dragon. You've been to the pit, haven't you?" I said. I didn't stop to wonder whether anyone had noticed him.

Soon Beatrice and I had both eaten our fill and we set off again. Torcher, carrying the rucksack in his mouth, led the way. To my surprise, he seemed to know that we were heading for the tall stone on the cliffs, and he kept looking back over his shoulder to make sure that we were following him.

At last we arrived at the stone, but it looked like someone had been there before us. We gazed about, perplexed by the scene in front of us: the ground was pockmarked with small pits and piles of earth.

"Someone's been digging," said Beatrice at last. I began to examine the stone more closely. There were shapes and symbols carved into it. Runes, I guessed, but in the middle was the symbol of a huge hammer.

"The Hammer of the Dragons!" I gasped.

"So that's what they were searching for." Beatrice nodded knowingly. Even the ground at the bottom of the stone had been scooped out. I was surprised it still stood upright.

Beatrice began sliding her hand over the runes, as if it would help her to clarify their meaning. She walked around the stone as she did so. Suddenly, she let out a gasp. "Daniel, I think there's a map scratched on this side. Maybe it's a map of the island!"

I hurried round to look. "You might be right," I replied. The rough scratching on the stone certainly looked like a map, and it was triangular, with a picture of something that could be a volcano in the middle. There were other marks, too, accompanied by more runic writing. I began to examine the runes, but to my disappointment, although I knew the shapes of the letters, I could not make head or tail of what they said. They had been written in a language that was neither English nor Dragonish.

"T-L-A-T-L-A," I said, reading what appeared to be a title above the map. "What does *tlatla* mean?"

"I've no idea," said Beatrice. "But it was the Vikings who

used runes, wasn't it? Maybe the Vikings came to this island. They might have put up the stone!"

"Unless we can decipher the runes, we'll never know," I replied. "Dr. Drake might have been able to read them, but we don't have a chance."

Beatrice looked thoughtful. "A dragon might be able to help. I'll bet that Idraigir can read Viking."

"Except he's not here," I said, a little impatiently. "And so it looks like we'll have to try to free a frost dragon, after all."

Beatrice sighed. "I suppose you're right. Torcher will have to show us the route he took to steal our lunch, won't you, Torcher?"

As Beatrice spoke, I noticed that Torcher had wandered away from the rune stone and was standing a few hundred yards closer to the edge of the cliffs that jutted out over the sea. He was waiting for us with an expectant expression.

"Hang on a moment, Beatrice. I don't think Torcher was leading us to the stone at all, were you, boy? It looks like he wants to take us back to Koa's lair. The tunnel entrance lies just on the other side of where he's sitting. Isn't that right, Torcher?"

"But why would he want to take us there?" exclaimed Beatrice. "From what you've told me, that's the last place we should be heading!"

"Come on, Torcher. Come back!" I shouted. "It isn't safe. We need your help to free a frost dragon so that we can find Idraigir."

But Torcher didn't shift an inch. Instead, he suddenly kneeled on the ground and started to cough.

We rushed over to him and Beatrice ran her fingers across his brow. "Alexandra's poisoned him!" she gasped. "Ugh, stand back, he's going to be sick!" Beatrice jumped back as Torcher began to retch.

I half turned away, not wanting to lay eyes on a pungent bubbling mess of dragon vomit, but to my astonishment, none came. Torcher coughed one final time, and out of his mouth popped a glistening gem, attached to a golden chain.

"It's the Dragon's Eye!" exclaimed Beatrice. "But how —?"

My heart was in my mouth as I picked it up and beheld Dr. Drake's dear, lost face fixed in the gem until such time as the dragons would choose a new Dragon Master. Now that Dr. Drake was gone, that time would not be long in coming. For a while I had been hoping that I might be the one to take on the role, but right now that idea made my stomach churn. I shuddered visibly. "Dr. Drake was carrying this with him. Torcher must have gone down into the crater to get it."

"So that's where you disappeared to, is it, Torcher?" Beatrice looked directly at the dragon chick. "You went back to find Dr. Drake!"

"But how did he get out again?" I wondered aloud. "Torcher, have you learned to fly?"

At that, Torcher spread out his wings and let out a roar.

Beatrice stared at him. I stared at him. I knew what she was going to ask, but I hardly dared to hope.

"Torcher, did Dr. Drake give you the gem? Or did you take it from him?"

"*Sssssorrr.*"

"Dr. Drake gave it to you!" Beatrice pointed to the doctor's face and mimed the action.

"*Sssssorrr.*"

Beatrice let out a cry. "So he's still alive?"

"*Sssssorrr!*"

If only it were true! But surely the little dragon did not know what he was saying. The crater was too hot, the poisonous smoke too thick. I had seen it for myself.

"But how can he be alive, Torcher?" I said, bewildered. I could feel the tears welling up in my eyes. "No one could survive a fall into a volcano. No one."

As if in answer, Torcher came up to me and took the Dragon's Eye gem carefully in his mouth.

"What are you doing?" I said frantically. "We have to save Dr. Drake!"

"Koa," said Torcher. "*Algrai* Koa. *Sssssorrr?*" My mouth fell open. Torcher had never before uttered more than one or two simple words in Dragonish. Looking back once, he waved his tail and disappeared over the edge of the cliff.

"No!" I screamed. "Torcher, no! You don't understand! Koa will kill us if we go down there. You can't take the Dragon's Eye to him! Please!"

But Torcher had gone.

There was a long silence. Beatrice touched my shoulder. "Daniel. I think we should—"

"Are you insane?" I snapped. "Koa threatened to kill me, remember? And he will kill you, too. He is a man-eater! His cave is full of children's skulls!"

"Come on, Daniel," she said gently. "Torcher has never let us down. In fact, he's saved us twice now. I think it's time we put our complete trust in him, don't you?"

CHAPTER EIGHT

AN ALLY

It is a sad but universal truth that the older a dragon gets
the less he is likely to trust the words of a human.

—— *Dr. Ernest Drake, Letters to a Young Dragonologist*

I grumbled and cursed, but Beatrice's logic was beyond reproach: Torcher had not saved us before in order to betray us to Koa now. Perhaps the skulls were the remains of child thieves who had tried to steal from his lair, I reasoned. But even so, the thought of facing the man-eater once more filled me with dread. We began clambering back down the sea cliff and dropped into the mouth of the tunnel that led to the dragon's lair. More rocks had fallen from the ceiling, and I picked my way quickly through darkness and rubble, my senses on high alert in case another earthquake should begin.

Beatrice turned to me as she reached the stairway at last.

"Should we ask him a riddle or offer him some treasure?"

I shook my head. "I don't think any of that works with Koa. He refused to take part in a riddle contest, and he wasn't interested in my dragon whistle. All he did was tell me to leave the island immediately on pain of death. We only have his word for it that he isn't going to hurt Torcher. How do we know he was telling the truth about that?"

"Because something is making Torcher trust him." Beatrice wrinkled her nose. "He has a strange smell, doesn't he? How old do you think he is?"

There was a noise in the cavern below. "I don't think this is quite the time for a dragonological discussion, Beatrice," I whispered.

"Is he hundreds of years old, do you think?"

"Well, yes. He's enormous."

"Do you think he's old enough to have been here when Beatrice Croke came to the island?"

"I doubt it. I think amphitheres live to only about two hundred and fifty."

"Maybe the ones on this island are different."

"Why do you say that?"

Beatrice shrugged. "I don't know, it's just a hunch. . . . I'm going to try something."

I followed her down the stairs and could not believe my ears when she called out the riddle that the S.A.S.D. used as one of its passwords:

"When a dragon flies,
He seeks it with his eyes,
When a dragon roars,
He holds it in his claws."

Why was she giving away our secrets? Surely she did not believe that Koa could have anything to do with our dragonological order? At first there was no reply. My eyes grew accustomed to the dim light, and I made out the shape of Torcher, standing a few feet away from us, and then Koa's round green eyes blinking at me in the gloom. My palms felt sweaty. Could Torcher have made a terrible mistake? My eyes alighted on the skulls near the entrance, some of them bearing the gashes of great claw marks.

"Boy," said the dragon quietly, "why have you brought another to my lair? Did I not tell you to leave this island upon pain of death?"

But before I could say anything or even begin to explain, Beatrice strode boldly forwards into the cavern. "Wise and mighty Koa, we are indeed deeply sorry to have intruded on the privacy of your lair, but we have a friend who is in great danger. We do not have much time and—"

"Silence!" roared Koa, so fiercely that I backed away, hoping that Beatrice would have the sense to follow. Koa uncoiled his tail so that it barred the way out. "I asked you a question, boy. Come closer!"

Shaking with fear, I stumbled forwards into the centre

of the huge cavern; the feathers of Koa's mane were fluffed out angrily.

"Closer still!" he ordered.

I took another step. Koa's eyes seemed to grow larger. But I had been hypnotised by a dragon before and had learned how to resist it by doing mathematical calculations in my head. I did not drop my gaze for an instant. I heard a new note of respect in his voice as he said, "Whether you will live or not depends on the answers that you give me now. Did I not order you to leave my island instantly?"

"Yes."

"And yet you chose to disobey me. Explain this." Koa lifted up a wing tip, so that I could see the Dragon's Eye, hanging on its chain. "I do not see your face in this gem, or that of this girl. Can you convince me that you are not thieves? For if that is the case, why did you not tell me at once that you had come to this island with a Dragon Master?"

"But it is the Dragon Master who is in danger — if he is still alive. We were brought here against our will. I did not tell you before because I feared you."

"And why did you fear me? Is it because you are a thief, after all?"

"No, of course not. It is because I know what happened to the other children."

"What other children?"

I gestured towards the skeletons. "The ones you ate."

"Koa? Eat humans? Faugh! The very thought of your bitter-tasting flesh disgusts me!"

"Then why did you kill them?"

"Those are not human remains," the great dragon scoffed. "They are the bones of apes."

I shook my head in disbelief. Had I been wrong about Koa all along? "Apes?" I looked at the skulls again and noticed for the first time the heavy browridges and the small braincases. I let out a long, relieved sigh, suddenly feeling that I could breathe again.

"Apes," repeated Koa, licking his lips. "But you did not come here to learn about my eating habits." He reared up. "You are right to fear me! How do I know that you did not steal this gem from the Dragon Master?"

Beatrice wrung her hands. "That is what we are trying to tell you. The Dragon Master, Dr. Drake, is our friend. He must have given Torcher the Dragon's Eye to bring to us, to prove that he is still alive. But he is in great danger, trapped inside the crater of the volcano. We have no time to waste."

"But Torcher did not give the Dragon's Eye to you, did he? He brought it to me."

"He was not supposed to," I explained.

Koa shook his head. "I think that you should give your dragon companion rather more credit. He knows—or guesses—who I am. He did well to bring the gem to me. The Dragon Master will be grateful to him." He let out a long breath and looked out of his cave towards the ocean. "So, a Dragon Master has come from across the sea. Perhaps this is the great danger that was spoken of. Perhaps the time of the prophecy is at hand!"

"What prophecy?" asked Beatrice. "What are you talking about?"

Koa turned back towards us; he was already uncoiling his vast bulk. "I shall explain it to you later, but now the time is short. If the Dragon Master is still alive, I shall find him." Koa began shifting about on his treasure hoard, as if getting ready for takeoff. He paused for a moment, and he turned again to me. "The answer to your riddle is 'treasure,' by the way. It is strange to hear my own riddle spoken back to me, after all these years."

"Your own riddle?" I was confused.

"Yes." I thought I caught the hint of a proud smile on Koa's face. "How much do you know about the Dragon's Eye?"

"Only what Dr. Drake has told us."

"Did he tell you that the gem came from this island?"

"No."

"Then study and learn. . . ." With that, Koa reached back his feathered head and blew out a column of brilliant blue fire that lit up the entire cavern. "Behold!" he cried, his eyes fixed on the wall at the back of the cave. I gasped in amazement. While the front half of the cave was formed from natural rock, the rear wall had been smoothed over and covered with a series of detailed frescoes, painted in exquisite colours.

The first showed an armoured woman kneeling as she offered a long-handled war hammer to an amphithere. From the pattern of its plumage, I guessed that this was the younger Koa. In the next, the same amphithere stood by a smoking volcano, holding in its mouth a gem. Inside the gem, I could just make out an image of the face of the armoured woman. The third showed the hammer in a cavern, with water flowing all around it.

The flame died in Koa's mouth and the images vanished.

Beatrice looked at me in wonder. "It's Beatrice Croke!" she exclaimed. "I never expected her to look like that! I always imagined her wearing a medieval dress, not a suit of armour!"

"So you were right, Beatrice. Koa is old enough to have met her. That must mean that Koa made the Dragon's Eye." I turned to Koa for confirmation, but he had already slithered soundlessly out of the cave and taken off. Now he was soaring away over the sea.

Beatrice watched him go with a puzzled look on her face. "But what do you think he meant about a prophecy?"

I shook my head. I did not know. My sister's hands were clenched into fists. She closed her eyes, as though she were praying. "Just please, please let him return with Dr. Drake."

Torcher padded over and nuzzled her comfortingly.

I patted him as I, too, gazed out to sea. "Don't worry, old

fellow," I said. "I'm sure Koa will find him and bring him back to us." But my certainty was baseless and I knew it.

We seemed to have been waiting in Koa's cave forever. As a full moon rose and the constellations twinkled over the silent ocean, neither of us spoke, caught up as we were in our desperate hopes—hopes that seemed wild and unjustified. I thought about my parents. I was certain Alexandra did not know what had happened to them, but that hardly meant that they were safe. And I thought of Erasmus, the valiant Dragon's Apprentice. Had he given his life to try to save ours? Or was he, at this moment, making his way across the Atlantic with Idraigir and a dragon army, coming to our rescue?

I stared forlornly out at the stars, and suddenly, my heart leapt, for winging its way towards us was a feathered, snake-like creature—it could only be Koa. At first I could not tell if there was anyone riding on his back, but Torcher let out a happy roar: his eyesight was far better than mine.

"It's Dr. Drake!" cried Beatrice. "He's alive!" But her excitement quickly faded as Koa came in to land; the figure that clung to him looked weak and ailing—a ghost of his former self.

I saw that his clothes were burned in places and that one arm was badly singed. His eyes were half closed and he was breathing with some difficulty. We found a smooth rock for the Dragon Master to rest upon, and Beatrice leaned

towards him, her face full of worry. "Is he going to be all right?" she whispered.

"It was a close-run thing," Koa answered. "He was trapped on a small ledge hidden from view, quite a distance above the lava, but he could not climb up and he would most certainly have perished had I not found him. There was another man near him, though he was dead, with a weapon in his hands."

Dr. Drake began coughing. I turned to look at him in alarm, but he waved his arm as if dismissing my concern. "It . . . was Shadwell!" he gasped. "Poor . . . foolish . . . devil. I think she set the Tunguskas on him and then . . . p-pushed him in."

Dr. Drake panted for breath, but though we begged him to rest, he insisted on recounting his story. Beatrice fetched him some water, and leaning up on one arm, he began to return to his old self. The Dragon Master explained that although the Tunguskas had hunted him, he had been hidden from view on the ledge, so they hadn't spotted him. "But then I heard a terrible bloodcurdling shriek, and it shook me to the core," he told us. "I hardly dared to look, for fear it might be one of you. You can imagine my relief when I saw it was Shadwell! Though, I feared that I, too, would end my days beside his body on that small ledge."

"Thank heavens Torcher found you," said Beatrice, delighted by the Dragon Master's newfound vigour.

"Thank heavens indeed," agreed Dr. Drake, raising his

cup of water to Torcher, who cocked his head on one side, proudly. "I gave him the Dragon's Eye so you two would know I had survived, and what a fortunate decision that was! If Koa had not fetched me, I should not have lasted much longer."

"Weren't the Tunguskas waiting for you when Koa carried you out?" I asked. "How did you escape them?"

"There was no need." Dr. Drake shrugged. "They were not there. I thought it strange at first, but Koa tells me there is a very good reason for it." He paused for a moment, to take another sip of water, and smiled, for the first time, seeing the looks of intrigue on our faces. "It seems that Tunguskas have a visual impairment, which I believe may also explain why Alexandra's ancestors found them impossible to train. Their eyesight during the day is as good as any dragon's, but at night they are very nearly blind. That is also why Koa has been able to stay here, even though Alexandra Gorynytchka's Tunguska army patrols the skies."

By now Koa had slithered past us and coiled up on his hoard. All at once, his voice boomed out, echoing around the cave. "It is not out of cowardice that I have allowed these Tunguska dragons the run of my island. I have been entrusted with a vitally important task. Long ago"—he paused and glanced around the cave to ensure that he had captured our attention—"this place was part of a much greater realm, where humans and dragons lived in harmony together. That realm was called . . ."

"Atlantis!" Beatrice and I almost squealed together, so delighted were we to discover that the legend might actually be true.

"That is correct." Koa nodded gravely, continuing with his story. "The humans lived in a great metropolis encircled by canals, while the dragons inhabited a subterranean city beneath the volcano, which we call fiery mountain, or *tlatla,* in Dragonish."

"*Tlatla!*" I gasped. "That's the name on the stone!"

"Correct again," affirmed Koa, though he looked a little irritated by my interruption. "When Atlantis was destroyed in a cataclysm, the human city sank beneath the waves of the sea, while the dragon city was buried beneath huge flows of mud and lava. Many dragons did survive — they could use the power of flight to escape the disaster, unlike the humans. They returned here, but their numbers soon dwindled, for the city was never rebuilt."

"And none of the humans survived?" asked Beatrice.

"Not one," answered Koa. "Though, humans did visit the island from time to time. Few of them proved friendly to dragons, however. Most treated us like brutes and tried to attack and drive us from our lairs.

"Then, one day, two knights landed upon the island in a ship with black sails. They were fleeing the wrath of their king. Unlike the other travellers, these visitors brought with them many dreadful weapons designed for the destruction or enslavement of dragons. It was not long before they began to use them. At first the dragons fought the knights, but alas, there was one dreadful weapon for which they were no match."

"I presume that was the Hammer of the Dragons?" I commented.

"Indeed." Koa nodded slowly. "Forged by a shaman from the icy wastes of the east, it had murderous properties that went far beyond anything we had encountered before. When its power was unleashed, it killed every single dragon on the island. Every mother, every father, every brother, every sister . . . All were slain and their bodies left to rot where they lay. All, that is, except two."

"You?" breathed Beatrice. "And . . ."

"My brother and I were away from the island when the battle took place. We returned to discover the terrible carnage and swore undying vengeance on the knights. We feared to attack them, for we did not know what terrible means they had used to slay our kinsfolk. But help and an explanation was not long in coming."

"Beatrice Croke!" I exclaimed. "Did she come with her son, Daniel?"

By way of an answer, Koa lit up the cave once more, and Dr. Drake gazed at the paintings with wonder in his eyes.

"Oh, my," said Dr. Drake. He lifted himself to his feet for the first time, and he drew closer to the wall to examine the pictures in more detail. "They're exquisitely beautiful."

"Daniel Croke was responsible for the paintings in this chamber," said Koa.

"If I've read them correctly," began Dr. Drake, "it looks as though Beatrice Croke helped you to defeat the Dragonsbane Knights who had ransacked your island, and then she hid the hammer, so the tragedy could not be repeated."

A wistful look came into the old dragon's eyes. "Beatrice Croke renewed my faith in humankind," he said. "That's why I made the Dragon's Eye for her. It was a symbol of a pact between dragonologists and dragons. I hoped it would be carried by her successors, so that dragons such as I would recognise them and help them in their time of need."

"I still do not understand how you avoided detection by the Tunguskas," said Beatrice. "Even if they can't see you at night, can't they smell you?"

"Ah, yes," said Koa. "But scents can be disguised. I have long concealed my existence from other dragons by using this substance." Koa gestured with a claw to a grey ball in the corner of the cave that looked like a large lump of dried clay.

"Ambergris!" exclaimed Dr. Drake.

I crossed the cave to inspect it. It was obvious now that this was the source of the strange smell that surrounded Koa and his cave. "Is it some sort of rock?"

"No. It is produced in the stomachs of whales. I am told

that some humans find the smell quite pleasant," said Koa. "Certainly, it is in plentiful supply on the beaches here, and it does seem to prevent the black dragons from showing any interest in my cave. They are, as you can see, remarkably stupid creatures. Unlike their formidable mistress, however, who appears almost diabolically intelligent."

"She's searching for the Hammer of the Dragons," I said.

"Yes, I believe that she knows where the hammer is concealed. But she does not know how to open the cavern, and I hope that she will never find that out. However, she does have another weapon at her disposal. She uses dragon dust to control her dragon army. Do you know of it?"

Beatrice nodded. "Yes, it is the dust that is produced by mother dragons when they are looking after their chicks."

"Indeed. Although it condenses from their breath, it takes a great deal of time — centuries, in fact — to build up in any quantity, and I believe that Alexandra Gorynytchka has nearly run out of it."

"Nearly run out of it!" Beatrice smiled, and I felt my heart leap. If only that were true!

"Why else would she risk everything to find more of it? She has used up what she had left to enslave the frost dragons. Cracking rock with fire and ice is the quickest way she has found to excavate the lost dragon city."

"So that's what they're searching for," I muttered to myself. Out loud, I asked, "Will there still be dragon dust there after all this time?"

"Oh, yes. When Alexandra Gorynytchka reaches the breeding chambers, she will find a vast quantity of dragon dust built up over millennia. With that, she could use her dragon army to create havoc for another hundred years. Then, she will turn her full attention to the Hammer of the Dragons."

Suddenly I realised that something had been troubling me. "But if the hammer was so dangerous, why didn't Beatrice Croke simply destroy it?"

"Because the prophecy prevented her," Koa answered flatly.

"A prophecy?" said Dr. Drake, raising an eyebrow.

"Indeed," said Koa gravely. "The prophecy is central to my role on this island. It was shown to me by Beatrice Croke herself, having been passed down from the hammer's own creator—a shaman from ancient times named Dobrinja—who bitterly regretted making the malevolent artefact.

"But what does the prophecy say?" It was Dr. Drake who spoke, but we were all on tenterhooks to know the answer.

Koa took his time. "In essence," he began at last, "the prophecy is this: the hammer is, for dragons, a terrible evil surpassing all others, but one day an evil will come to match it. Those two evils can be destroyed together, but not apart. If either is absent, then the one that remains will spell doom for all dragons and their utter destruction. So, according to the prophecy, the hammer must be preserved and kept hidden until that other evil manifests itself."

"But what has this got to do with Dr. Drake?"

"The prophecy also states that two humans, knowledgeable in the ways of dragons, will do battle for the hammer. One—the evil one I spoke of—will bring an army of slaves, and her helpers will be wicked men; the other—who will come to save the dragons—will bring an army of free creatures, and his helpers will be but children, wise beyond their years in the ways of dragons."

"So you're saying that Alexandra Gorynytchka is one, and the other is Dr. Drake?"

"From the Dragon's Eye gem, I can see that Dr. Drake is the successor of Beatrice Croke, for his image has been fixed in the gem. And not only that—what has convinced me most of all is that the Dragon Master has arrived here with two children who seem to know so much about dragons."

"It is utterly remarkable to think that a Dragon Master should bear such great responsibility and yet know nothing about it," Dr. Drake said, looking thoughtful. "How did Beatrice Croke learn of the prophecy herself?"

"The hammer is accompanied by an anvil of black crystal that is etched all over with runic writing describing the full nature of the hammer," Koa explained.

I shivered. "And what is your role in all of this?" I asked.

"I am the herald of the army of free dragons. My task is to witness the unfolding of the prophecy, to keep the memory of the prophecy alive, and to summon the army when the time comes. I may also assist the one who has come to save the dragons, with such help and information as I can. That task was originally bequeathed to my brother, but, alas, he is no longer here."

Dr. Drake nodded gravely. "And how is the prophecy to be fulfilled?"

"You must use the hammer to oppose Alexandra Gorynytchka, so that the two evils can cancel each other out. The hammer must first be taken from the cavern where it is kept. But that will not be easy."

Beatrice folded her arms and looked at Koa intently. "So you know where the cavern is?"

"Of course. Come with me before dawn breaks tomorrow and I will show you. Tonight you may rest here. Have you food and drink?"

"We still have some leftovers from the pack Torcher brought us," I said.

"Then get some rest. The Dragon Master and I have many things that we must discuss together before the sun rises."

CHAPTER NINE
THE DRAGON ARENA

Even Roman historians such as Tacitus, while giving an enthusiastic
account of the bloodthirsty German wars, preferred to omit from his
annals a mention of Rome's disgraceful treatment of dragons.

—— *Dr. Ernest Drake, Letters to a Young Dragonologist*

When Dr. Drake woke us it was still dark. Beatrice and I clambered groggily onto Koa's back. We must have looked a comical sight, with Dr. Drake near Koa's head, myself and Beatrice in the middle, and Torcher clinging on, near the end, to the great dragon's tail. The amphithere flew us smoothly to the volcanic peak, and after circling a few times, he descended into a steep-sided jungle valley. We landed by a pool at the bottom of a roaring waterfall, and I shuddered; our location seemed eerily familiar.

"Beatrice, isn't this where we ended up yesterday, after we jumped off the cliff?" I asked.

"I think so, but I don't remember seeing a cavern anywhere," Beatrice answered.

"That is because the entrance is hidden on a high ledge behind that waterfall," said Koa. "It is a natural cave, but it has been sealed with an indestructible door that can only be opened with a secret key."

"So it is possible to climb up there?" Beatrice queried as she peered up at the torrent of roaring water, craning her neck and squinting up into the darkness.

"Quite impossible unless you are a spider. But it can be accessed from above. I have seen men being lowered down on ropes. One of Miss Gorynytchka's companions is a dwarf dragon to whom the cliffs present no obstacle. He has been helping the men in their search." An image of the beastly Flitz came into my mind. I tried not to think about the vicious little dragon.

"So Alexandra knows the location of the cave?" asked Dr. Drake, a little alarmed.

"Do not fear," said Koa. "Even if she finds the door, she will never be able to open it. Only a Dragon Master can do that."

I peered up eagerly into the darkness. "Can either of you see anything?"

"Wait," said the amphithere. "In a moment the sun will rise. Then I shall fly you up there and you will see it properly."

Koa carried us to a point halfway up the waterfall and hovered. Now the stars were fading and the sun had appeared above the horizon, filling the gorge with light and colour. I gasped, for now I could see a ledge and beyond it a tall arched doorway hidden behind the rushing waters that had been invisible from the ground. But instead of landing, to my surprise, Koa turned and flew out of the gorge a long way down the flank of the volcano to an old ruin. Curved tiers of seats rose from a huge semicircular platform, and in the centre of the topmost tier was a ruined building like a stone pavilion. To my amazement I saw that it was crowned with statues of an amphithere and a European dragon, locked in mortal combat.

As soon as Koa landed, we dismounted, and Torcher immediately began nosing his way through the ruins.

"Is this place safe?" I asked anxiously, for by now it was near daylight and I would not have been at all surprised had a party of guards stepped out to arrest us.

"I cannot smell either humans or dragons here," said Koa. "But you must keep moving: nowhere on this island will be safe for long. Alexandra is sure to have sent out hunting parties to look for you. Our only advantage lies in the fact that she almost certainly believes that the Dragon Master has perished."

"But what is this place?" asked Beatrice. "It looks like a Roman amphitheatre."

"That is exactly what it is," affirmed Koa. "It is a dragon arena."

"A dragon arena?" I looked at the duelling statues and felt a thrill of excitement, imagining the spectacle of two

magnificent dragons in single combat. Then I noticed Torcher sniffing at the statues uneasily, and I was filled with shame. How could I ever enjoy a contest that would inevitably result in a dragon's death?

"So what is it that we are to do here?" asked Dr. Drake.

"This is where you must begin your quest to obtain the Hammer of the Dragons. Beatrice Croke feared that, over the centuries, the Dragon Masters might become corrupted by their power and knowledge. And so, she set a series of tests that the Dragon Master must pass before he or she could open the cave to release the hammer."

"Can't you open the cave?" Beatrice asked Koa, surprised.

"Beatrice Croke decided that none but the one spoken of in the prophecy should have the power to open it; one who she believed was almost certain to be a Dragon Master. She hid clues to the whereabouts of a secret key.

"In the twelve thousand years since Atlantis was destroyed, four peoples have sent explorers to visit the island. All four are represented now only by the ruins that they left behind. One clue is hidden among the ruins left by each of those peoples," Koa explained.

Dr. Drake smiled. "The Greek philosopher Plato estimated that the destruction of Atlantis took place just over nine thousand six hundred years before his time. It seems he was correct!" He shielded his eyes and gazed around. "Are all of the clues on this island?"

"Yes. There are four places you must search: this dragon arena is one. It dates from the time of the Roman emperor Caesar Augustus. Next you must visit a rune stone erected by the followers of a Viking named Thorstan. Third is a pyramid that dates from the time of the Aztecs, and, finally, the mausoleum built by Beatrice Croke herself, to house the fallen bodies of the knights who brought the Hammer of the Dragons here."

"How shall we recognise the clues?" I asked.

"That is for you to discover, but one clue will lead you on to the next," answered Koa.

"Surely we don't have time for all this?" said Beatrice. "You know the danger posed by Alexandra Gorynytchka. If you know where the key is, why do you not simply tell us rather than wasting time?"

Koa flicked his tail. "Because I do not know. I created the Dragon's Eye gem, but it was my brother who made the unbreakable door that bars the cavern, and it was Beatrice Croke and her son, Daniel, who fashioned the lock and prepared the clues. Beatrice was adamant that none must lay their hands on the Hammer of the Dragons, save he who is named in the prophecy. If the hammer were released too soon, it would only wreak evil, or else be destroyed before its time, leaving dragons to look forward to a future of bleak destruction."

Dr. Drake looked grim. "While we are searching for the clues, will you stay here to keep watch for us?"

"I cannot. Now that the workings of the prophecy have begun, I must do what I can to summon an army of free dragons. But it will not be easy."

Suddenly I had an idea. "Why don't you fly to Britain?" I suggested. "Idraigir and the British dragons will be anxious to help, and you can let them know what has happened to us."

"Then that is where I shall go first," said Koa. "I shall seek out the dragon called the Wantley Dam. It has been many centuries since I have seen or spoken to her."

"Then, alas, I have tragic news for you," said Dr. Drake. "She was brutally slain by the same enemy that we face here. Idraigir is the Guardian Dragon now."

Koa moaned. "That is grievous news indeed. She was a steadfast friend and ally."

"She died defending the Dragon's Eye," said Dr. Drake. "These children bore witness to her bravery, and her passing was mourned by many."

"Then let her death be not in vain!" Koa raised his voice boldly. "I shall seek out Idraigir. I shall return to you with help."

"Will you go only to Britain?" I asked. "Or will you seek for help elsewhere? Panthéon and his gargouilles in Paris would be willing to join you. And I am sure that wyverns, such as Uwassa, and hydras, such as Faki-Kifa-Kafi, would do anything if it meant the defeat of Alexandra Gorynytchka. Not to mention the *lung* in China."

"I shall send word via the Dragon Vine for all the help I can muster," replied Koa.

"May I ask of you one further favour?" Dr. Drake began. "When you reach Britain and find Idraigir, can you discover what happened to his apprentice, Erasmus?" asked Dr. Drake.

Koa raised his feathery eyebrows. "Erasmus?" he queried, inclining his head a little.

"He is our friend," explained Beatrice. "He fell, trying to defend us from the Tunguskas when they kidnapped us."

"Then I shall certainly find out what happened to him. And now, I must leave you and bid you good luck."

"Wait," cried Beatrice. "How long will you be gone, and how on earth shall we survive without you?"

Koa was readying himself for takeoff, but he paused for a moment, then said, "Before I go I shall bring you some provisions and leave them near that building." Koa indicated the stone ruin. "You will need to fortify yourselves for the conflicts that lie ahead."

While Koa had been speaking, Dr. Drake had been deep in thought, but now he turned to the amphithere with a serious expression. "Koa, I must ask you to take Daniel and Beatrice with you, now, back to Britain. Will you do that for me?"

For an instant I thought I had misheard him. Was it possible? After everything that we had been through, everything that we had done, Dr. Drake was actually sending us away? But surely he didn't mean to fight Alexandra and her brutal minions by himself? "You cannot do this on your own," I blurted.

"And the prophecy says that you need children as your helpers," said Beatrice.

But Dr. Drake's face was set. "Whatever the prophecy says, I cannot allow it. It is too dangerous."

"I will do anything else you request in order to counter this evil, but I cannot take the children," said Koa, relaxing again from takeoff position. "The prophecy is specific on this matter. Without them you would not have survived. What's more, they have already played a large part in fulfilling the prophecy. For better or worse, they must see this quest through to the end."

Dr. Drake turned to us with a frown and hesitated. "I hate to put you in such danger, but it seems that I have no choice. In some ways I fear for what might happen to you, for you have seen how terrible that woman can be, but in other ways"—and here he gave a relieved grin—"in other ways, I shall be delighted to have the help of such able assistants. After all, you have already proved your worth in the unravelling of dragonological clues more times than I can remember."

Koa, having little patience for the discussion, readied himself once more for the off.

Beatrice turned and spotted him. "Will you bring us

word of our parents?" she asked. "They also went missing the day that we were kidnapped."

"I will do what I can," replied Koa, his voice fading quickly as he rose ever higher into the sky; his final word sounded like little more than a whisper. "Farewell!"

Koa circled the arena and flew off in the direction of the sea. They watched him for a while, until Dr. Drake let out a heavy sigh. "Let us begin," he said. "We must make haste."

"But where should we start?" I asked.

"Let us see," Dr. Drake began, stroking his chin thoughtfully. "If Torcher remains alert for intruders, we can spread out and see what we can find. We need to look for inscriptions, pictures, runes. Anything that appears out of place in a Roman arena."

"But what do you think about this whole prophecy business?"

"Prophecies are strange things. They can often come true in ways that we do not expect. Besides, contrary to whatever Koa says, my arrival here may be pure coincidence, although I admit to being greatly intrigued by the connections between this island and the Secret and Ancient Society of Dragonologists."

The more I thought about it, the more remarkable it seemed that we were standing in a place where our distant ancestor Beatrice Croke had left clues for us centuries before. As I surveyed the ruins, I hoped that we would be able to recognise those clues when we saw them.

There were vast stone steps leading down from the centre of the stage. Dr. Drake explained that in Roman times, they were probably covered with a wooden trapdoor and would have led to the beast pens beneath. They looked dragon size, and Torcher sniffed at them suspiciously.

A shiver ran down my spine. "Do you think it was dragon versus dragon, or were the dragons pitted against humans?"

"Didn't the Romans execute Christians by throwing them to wild animals?" observed Beatrice.

"You both have very vivid imaginations," said Dr. Drake matter-of-factly. "But before we venture underground, perhaps we should investigate the open areas." He gestured towards the stone pavilion. Despite the thrill I felt at the challenge of solving the ancient puzzle, time very definitely was not on our side. It was clear that Alexandra Gorynytchka would stop at nothing to prevent us from finding the hammer, and—according to her—the island itself might be destroyed at any moment by a volcanic eruption.

I followed Beatrice and Dr. Drake into the ruined building. Beatrice was already inside, studying a carved stone throne intently. "Have you found anything?" I asked.

"Nothing," she said disconsolately, "except that." She looked up and pointed at the ceiling. Much of it had fallen in and was open to the sky, but on the remaining section there was a faded painting of an arena, just like the one we were standing in. Three gladiators—one with a net and two with swords—were engaged in combat with a fire-breathing amphithere. The swordsmen stood back-to-back, while the man with the net was lying injured on the ground. Above them, the emperor, wearing a purple toga, was giving a thumbs-down sign.

As I looked at the place where the emperor was sitting I realised something, but Beatrice got there before me.

"It's a painting of this arena!" she exclaimed. "You can see the outline of the volcano in the background."

"And look," I said. "Some of the seats have symbols on them." I pointed to a golden cross, a horse, a dagger, and a five-pointed star. "Could they be a clue of some kind?"

Dr. Drake studied them closely. "If they are clues," he said, "then I fear we do not have the means to interpret them. I suspect that these are the symbols of some of the great aristocratic families of Rome."

Just at that moment, Torcher appeared in the doorway.

"Guskas," he said, casting an anxious glance over his shoulder.

A line of Tunguskas were travelling in our direction, overhead. They were some distance away, but it would not be long before they reached us. I felt relieved that we weren't out in the open, and I quickly crouched down next to the others.

"Won't they see us?" Beatrice sounded panicky.

"They are flying very low," said Dr. Drake. "I think we need to hide somewhere else. Quickly, follow me."

He led us out of the pavilion and down the steps that disappeared under the stage. We found ourselves in a wide corridor that gave access to a series of caves. As my eyes adjusted to the dim light, I could just make out a dragon-size drinking trough in the largest cave at the farthest end, next to the rusted remains of a huge metal bolt in the wall.

"These must have been the dragon pens." I had whispered it, but even so, my voice echoed around the empty chambers.

"Look at this!" hissed Beatrice. She had gone farther into the cave and was pointing at something on the wall. "I've found some drawings. Do you think they were made by dragons?"

"It is possible," said Dr. Drake, looking across from the other side of the corridor.

"And there is some writing here, too," she said, beckoning us over. "Can you translate it, Dr. Drake?"

The Dragon Master looked at it and frowned. "I am afraid not. I have never even seen this script before. From the form of the letters, it looks like a cross between Sumerian cuneiform and ancient Aztec."

"Perhaps it is ancient Atlantean—from the peoples of the city of Atlantis," I suggested.

"It doesn't look twelve thousand years old," scoffed

Beatrice. "That's how old it would need to be if the citizens all perished with their city."

"Then maybe it's Roman," I ventured. "The Romans lived only about two thousand years ago."

Dr. Drake smiled. "Of course, these texts may have been scratched here by captive ampthitheres. But if that were the case, I am afraid it would not help us in our quest, for I am sure that Beatrice Croke would not have written clues in ancient Atlantean."

"So what must we do?" asked Beatrice.

"We must keep searching," replied Dr. Drake.

I found some more etchings on the wall. "These pictures over here are without any writing." I pointed to them. "Do you think the dragons might have scratched those?"

"Let me see." Dr. Drake stood back so that he could examine them more clearly. "The workmanship is rather primitive compared to the other pictures, isn't it? But I think you might be on to something. There seem to be two pictures: one of a flying dragon and one of a dragon asleep."

"Oh, and look, there is another group of pictures down here," I said. "A cup, a sword, a box, some coins. It must be a dragon's treasure. But why are they all marked with a star?"

"Look!" Suddenly Beatrice's arm shot up. High on the wall was a picture of a book with a dragon curled around it: the symbol of the Secret and Ancient Society of Dragonologists.

"So these pictures must have been left here by Beatrice Croke!" I said. "But what do they mean?"

Beatrice thought for a moment and grinned. "I think I know!" she cried. "It's the S.A.S.D. password, isn't it? When a dragon flies . . . ?"

"He seeks it with his eyes!" I was jumping with excitement.

"And when a dragon roars . . . ?"

"He holds it in his claws! Of course! This is the riddle that Koa said was his. And we know that the answer is 'treasure,' but the problem is, how do we find it?"

"I think I can guess," said Dr. Drake. "There's a clue in the ceiling painting we saw in the pavilion."

"What do you mean?" asked Beatrice.

"It's the star!" I cried. "It's the star symbol, isn't it? All we need to do is to find out exactly which seat the star is on in the painting, then find the seat that matches it in the arena. Beatrice Croke's clue will be there!"

There was no sign of any Tunguskas as we left the safety of the underground chambers and hurried back to the stone pavilion. But before we reached it, Dr. Drake held up his hand.

"Wait," he said. He pointed to a small handcart next to the entrance. Torcher was already scampering enthusiastically towards it and I quickly guessed why.

"It's Koa," I said. "These are the provisions he promised. He must have left them while we were down in the caves."

I was right: there were leather bottles full of water, and sacks containing ship's biscuits, a few oranges, and some cheese. Not the most exciting fare, but certainly enough to keep us going.

Inside the pavilion a brief inspection of the mural showed that the star was inscribed on the ninth seat from the end in the bottom row. But when we tried to find the actual seat, we encountered a problem. None of the real seats had any visible markings on them, and parts of the arena had crumbled away, so it was impossible to identify one specific seat.

"What if there isn't a marking? What if the clue is simply hidden underneath the seat?" Beatrice had hold of the stone slab that formed the base of one of the seats and was trying vainly to lift it.

But even with the help of myself and Dr. Drake, it took an age to slide the heavy slab onto the floor. Underneath was nothing more than earth and rock.

I stepped back and examined the seats again. "These are dragonological clues, aren't they?" I mused. "So perhaps the ninth scat does have a special marking on it, but you need dragon fire to reveal it."

No sooner had Torcher played a jet of flame across the backs of the seats, than the unmistakable shape of a star began to glow on one of them. We lifted up the base together, and I grinned at the others triumphantly as we uncovered a neat recess in which nestled an ancient-looking parchment.

"This is remarkable," said Dr. Drake as he held it up to examine it. "It has been some time since I came across a piece of draccum."

"Draccum? What's that?" asked Beatrice.

"It is a medieval parchment made from the shed skin of a young amphithere," he explained.

"But it's blank!" I was terribly disappointed.

"Not totally," said Beatrice, pointing to what looked like a smudge at the top of the parchment. "There's a tiny picture of an eye just there."

"My goodness, Beatrice!" exclaimed Dr. Drake. "I'd nearly missed that."

"But it's just a picture of an eye." I shrugged. "A dragon's eye."

"By Jove, Daniel, I think you might be right!" cried Dr. Drake.

I was dumbfounded. "What do you mean?"

With a flourish, Dr. Drake produced the Dragon's Eye gem from his waistcoat pocket and held it up to his eye, using it like a lens to peer at the parchment.

"It works!" he exclaimed. "How intriguing. Ebenezer Crook always claimed that this gem possessed secrets of which we were unaware. Here"—he passed me the gem—"look through that and tell me what you see."

I couldn't see anything.

"Try rotating the gem slightly," advised Dr. Drake.

As I did so a fine script suddenly appeared on the parchment. "It's a message!" I exclaimed, hardly able to control my excitement. "It must be from Beatrice Croke—the handwriting is very old-fashioned, but I think I can make it out."

"Read it out!" urged Beatrice, almost jumping up and down with delight.

"To my eminent and esteemed successor. I urge you to caution, for the time of the Dobrinja's prophecy is upon you, and a great danger threatens those we hold dear. You shall learn more as you uncover the clues. They will lead you to the key that unlocks the cave wherein you will find the Hammer of the Dragons. You need to find ten letters, the first of which is given by this riddle:

> *I am in heart and also brain,*
> *But not in body, blood, or vein,*
> *I am in water, also bread,*
> *But not in drinking, food, or fed.*

You will find the site of the next clue in the following verse:

> *Wave-wandering men set up a stone,*
> *Upon a cliff where wild winds moan.*

It tells a tale of times of old,
Beneath, three letters you'll behold.

Go with dragon speed!

Beatrice Croke."

I returned the Dragon's Eye to Dr. Drake. "The verse must refer to the rune stone near Koa's cave," I said.

"But that's on the other side of the pit where the dragons are working," said Beatrice.

"And not entirely detrimental to our cause," said Dr. Drake resolutely. "It is high time that I saw this pit for myself."

"But isn't it too dangerous?" Just thinking about the place brought me out in a cold sweat.

"Well, certainly I would not like to cross too much open country while the Tunguskas are searching for you—and I would like to keep the fact that I am alive a secret for as long as possible. But I fear that with time pressing upon us, we have little choice." He paused for a moment, considering our options. "I think, however, that we should wait in the caves here until dusk, at least. We can entertain ourselves with Beatrice Croke's first riddle as we wait."

CHAPTER TEN

THE LOST CITY

Sometimes it feels to me as though all modern dragonological discoveries are mere postscripts to the knowledge acquired in a far-distant time when dragons and humans lived side-by-side in peace, knowledge passed down to us piecemeal as dragon myth and legend.

—— *Dr. Ernest Drake, Letters to a Young Dragonologist*

I t did not take us long to determine that the answer to the first riddle was the letter *A*. After that we had little to do but sit impatiently on our hands until darkness fell and we were safe from the Tunguskas.

The moon provided us with enough light to cross the volcanic landscape without incident, but Dr. Drake's face was grim as he surveyed the long rows of sleeping dragons imprisoned in the pit, slumped in their chains as they rested from their daily toil.

Beatrice bit her lip. "I can't bear it. I just want to set them free," she said.

Dr. Drake shook his head sadly. "You have expressed my feelings exactly. But at present we cannot deviate from our

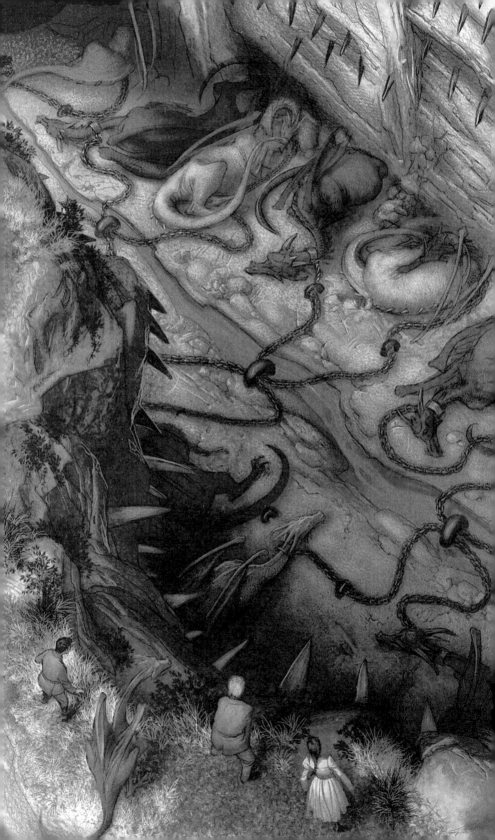

quest. If we succeed in that, then we will rescue all of them. We should continue on swiftly to the rune stone. Though I must admit, now that I have seen the pit for myself, I do not know how we are going to get to the other side. The land is too steep one way, and if we go the other way, we will have to cross miles of open country. Sooner or later, we will run into guards."

"Then we are completely stuck," exclaimed Beatrice despondently.

"The dragons are sleeping now, aren't they?" I said. "So perhaps there is another way through."

Beatrice looked at me with wide eyes. "Surely you aren't suggesting we go through the pit, Daniel?"

Dr. Drake stroked his moustache thoughtfully. "I think Daniel may be right. Sometimes the least likely option is the one that leads to greatest success. If you look carefully, you will see; the guards tend to patrol the perimeter — not the heart of their camp."

By now the last signs of activity in the pit were coming to an end. Even the men had piled up their tools and dragged away the last of the carts. Perhaps we would be able to sneak past the sleeping dragons without waking them, but we had only just started our descent to the pit when we heard voices approaching from below. I froze. Alexandra Gorynytchka appeared. She was talking with a man who, from the way he was dressed, looked like he was the pit foreman, and was followed by Flitz and six guards. It was impossible to hear what was being said, but Alexandra was smiling excitedly and clapping her hands. What if they had found the dragon dust that she was looking for already? I crept forwards, trying to hear.

"Stay back, Daniel!" hissed Dr. Drake.

Suddenly, to my horror, the rock I was leaning on slipped and tumbled down the slope, cracking and echoing as it fell. As it reached the bottom, a ghastly silence descended over the pit. Alexandra and her men turned and watched it roll to a stop.

"For goodness' sake, Daniel!" whispered Beatrice. "They'll see us."

"Quick!" hissed Dr. Drake. "Follow me!"

As we scrambled away from the edge of the pit, a party of Alexandra's men began lumbering up the slope. But Flitz was quicker than the lot of them—and now he was nearly upon us.

I clutched Beatrice's arm. "If Flitz spots Dr. Drake, then Alexandra will know that he's still alive."

Beatrice nodded. "What can we do?"

"Let's try to lead him the other way."

We moved to put our plan into action, but it seemed that Torcher had ideas of his own, as usual. The little chick let out an angry roar and sprang at the dwarf dragon. Flitz gave a screech and met Torcher in midair. The pair tumbled to the ground, where they began to fight with tooth and claw, nipping and tearing and sending out wicked little jets of flame. But after only a few seconds, Torcher got the better of Flitz and pinned him down. He looked up impatiently.

"Algrumble!" he croaked. *"Algrumble! Algrumble!"*

"What's he saying?" I asked Beatrice. By now Alexandra's men were nearly at the top of the slope.

"Fly!" exclaimed Beatrice. "It means 'fly.' I think he wants us to go. He's got control of Flitz for the moment, and he's trying to stop him from catching sight of you-know-who."

"But what if Alexandra's men catch Torcher?"

Beatrice pulled me away. "They won't catch him. He's too clever for that. They are after us, remember?"

Reluctantly, I followed Beatrice, and soon we came upon Dr. Drake, who looked grumpy and out of breath.

"I thought I told you two to follow me!" he cried.

"Torcher got into a fight with Flitz," I gasped. "We didn't want Flitz to see that you were all right. But the guards are right behind us, so we tried to put them off your trail."

"Well, that was good of you," admitted Dr. Drake hurriedly. He added sharply, "Now, follow me and don't hang back."

Dr. Drake suddenly veered away to the left and we chased after him. I heard shouts that were frighteningly close, and then, a moment later, we were running back towards the pit.

"Why are we going this way?" asked Beatrice.

Dr. Drake put a finger to his lips.

"We still need to get to the other side, don't we?" he whispered.

"What about Torcher?" asked Beatrice, alarmed.

"He will find us. Trust me."

We were now at the top of the slope again. Alexandra and her men were nowhere to be seen, and I looked over my shoulder, half expecting them to burst out from behind a rock. Anxiously, I followed Beatrice and Dr. Drake, who were clambering down into the pit. At the bottom, the slumbering forms of chained beasts surrounded us: pale frost dragons and black Tunguskas. I would never have a better opportunity to find out if frost dragons felt cold to the touch. I couldn't resist, and I put out my hand.

"Stop, Daniel!" Dr. Drake hissed urgently, under his breath. "You must not wake them, or we shall be discovered. Your insatiable curiosity has already caused enough mischief for one night." I pulled back my arm sheepishly.

A moment later, Torcher appeared at the top of the ridge, looking very pleased with himself. He spread out his little wings.

"No, Torcher!" whispered Beatrice, but the dragon chick could not hear her. He launched himself into the air and managed to glide for a few seconds before quickly losing height and bouncing off the steep slope, causing a miniature avalanche of rocks. He flapped his wings and, to my amazement, actually flew for a few yards, but the damage had been done. A shout went up and Alexandra's furious face appeared at the top of the pit. She was looking straight at us, her angry mouth forming an astonished *O*.

"It's Drake," she screamed. "He's alive! You let him past, you fools! Now, get him, and this time, don't let him go!"

With Torcher beside us we fled as fast as we could towards the far side of the pit, jumping and clambering over the chains that held the dragons. Alexandra's men were leaping down the slope, and when more guards appeared from another direction, we were cut off.

"We're never going to make it!" wailed Beatrice; even Dr. Drake had turned pale.

The nearest guards were almost upon us. They were brandishing weapons. We were as good as captured . . . or were we? I knew they wanted Dr. Drake alive, so I decided to take a chance. My hand had come to rest on my dragon whistle. I had no idea whether it would work, but—*pheeeep!*

I blew three loud blasts.

A moment later pandemonium erupted. The dragons around us awoke and leapt, roaring, to their feet. Encouraged, I blew another, harsher note, and the dragons began to panic, rearing up and pulling this way and that as they tried to escape from the chains that now whipped around them, threatening to decapitate anyone who got too close.

So the dragon whistle could counter the effects of dragon dust! That was quite a discovery. I had no idea how long it would last, but I kept on blowing, and soon our pursuers were lost behind a writhing wall of frantic creatures. Torcher's eyes, too, were wild and staring, and Beatrice and Dr. Drake were having to half carry, half drag him along.

"This way!" commanded Dr. Drake, pulling the dragon chick towards the excavations. I ran ahead, still blowing the whistle, and the panicking mass of dragons parted, allowing us to pass. In the distance I could just see Alexandra, her arms outstretched, her face contorted with rage, as she tried to regain control of the unruly beasts.

"Inside," said Dr. Drake as he disappeared through a low entrance in the rocky wall. His hand reached out and passed us two torches that he had picked up from a stack just inside the door.

Torcher, alert and back to his old self suddenly, gave two fiery breaths, and the brands were lit. It quickly became clear that the tunnel was much larger than it had at first appeared. Next to the stack of torches was a pile of wooden boxes and several coils of fuse wire.

I held up my dragon whistle. "Now that we have discovered what it can do, we could use it to free the whole army!"

Dr. Drake shook his head firmly. "The effect is based on surprise," he explained. "It doesn't last much longer than the whistle blast, I'm afraid. Look, Torcher is back to normal already."

As if to underline the point, Torcher was already scampering ahead of us into the tunnel—and looking round to make sure that we were following him.

"So it won't be long before Alexandra gets the dragons back under control," said Beatrice miserably. "Then they'll be after us again."

"Not if they can't see in the dark," I said.

"They can smell in the dark," said Dr. Drake. "But perhaps we can do something to delay them. Here, help me move some of these crates over to the entrance."

As I picked up the first crate, I saw, stamped in large black letters, the word 'dynamite.' Surely Dr. Drake didn't plan on burying us alive?

"Now, you two, move farther up the tunnel," he said when we had finished. "I shall follow you shortly."

We left Dr. Drake unrolling the coil of fuse wire, and a few moments later, I heard shouts coming from outside the cave. For a second I thought that Alexandra's men had caught him, then I saw a sudden bright flash and heard hurried footsteps echoing inside the tunnel. Dr. Drake had lit the fuse with his torch, and now he was running towards us.

"Look lively!" he cried. "Get as far away as you can and cover your ears."

We sprinted deeper into the tunnel, but we were hardly quick enough, for the next moment there was a deafening explosion, followed by a shock wave that sent me sprawling

across the floor, with Torcher on top of me. I scrambled up with the smell of dynamite in my nostrils and looked back. The entrance had vanished under a fall of rock.

"I hope there is more than one way out!" said Beatrice in alarm.

"So do I," replied Dr. Drake. "Though, Alexandra's men will open up that entrance again soon enough. The rockfall ought to hold them off just long enough to give us a head start out through the dragon city."

"I'd hardly call it a city," muttered Beatrice as we hurried along the rough-hewn tunnel.

"This is just one of the access tunnels," said Dr. Drake as we reached an archway. He swept back his arm, gesturing into the dark void beyond. "If I am right, the lost city of dragons lies on the other side, through that archway."

I raised my torch and gasped. Before us lay a cavern of immeasurable size, its domed roof decorated with what looked like thousands of twinkling stars. These stars were, in fact, precious stones glistening with the reflected light from our torches. Dotted around the cavern were enormous, life-size dragon statues, and in the centre, an imposing fountain dominated the entire scene. A myriad of small channels, which had once carried the water away from the fountain, ran in shallow grooves across the floor.

"So dragons really were civilised once," Beatrice commented, awestruck, as she gazed around the cavern in wonder.

"But their civilisation came to a gruesome end," said Dr. Drake, bringing us back to reality with a bump. He pointed to a pair of ornate golden doors that had been utterly crushed under a ton of rock. To the side, there was a wide section in the wall where lava had broken through and solidified into a twisted mass. A thick carpet of cinders lay on the floor. I imagined the horror of the final eruption. The lava flows must have been accompanied by deadly gases and choking black dust. I was sure I'd heard of something like that before.

I strolled up to one of the life-size dragon statues and lifted my torch. I very nearly dropped it again in shock. I had expected to see a creature that looked fine and noble, but instead the statue was of a young dragon curled into a tight ball, its head stretched back in an excruciating rictus of pain. Of course! The classics master at school had told me about the Roman city of Pompeii. It had been destroyed by the eruption of the volcano Vesuvius. I had seen plaster casts in London of some of the unlucky citizens preserved forever in agonised attitudes of death. This dragon wasn't a statue at all, but the fossil of a female amphithere that had died some twelve thousand years ago! She must have fled here in a bid to escape, and died when the doors collapsed, suffocating and then petrifying under an unforgiving blanket of volcanic dust.

There was a distant sound of smashing rocks. "Come on,

we must keep moving," said Dr. Drake. He pointed across the chamber. "My guess is that the largest tunnel on the other side will be the thoroughfare that leads into the heart of the city."

"A sort of dragon High Street," said Beatrice with a nervous laugh.

A few moments after we set off, there was a terrifying tremor as the earth began to shake. It lasted for only a few moments, but my sense of relief at this was short-lived. A few hundred yards farther on, just as we entered another huge cavern cut in two by a gigantic chasm, I heard a roar from somewhere behind us.

"Tunguskas!" I shouted.

"They've broken in!" cried Beatrice, looking around wildly.

"I feared as much," said Dr. Drake. "We need to get across this chasm."

"But how?" I cried. The roars were already growing louder.

"There!" said Beatrice. "There is a lever in the wall. Perhaps it lets down a bridge or something."

It took all four of us to pull on the lever before it began to move. There was a click as machinery started to clatter into motion. But instead of a bridge, as we had each hoped for, a circular contraption, which looked exactly like the wheel of a water mill, swung down from a recess above our heads. There were huge handles on each side of it, but they were so high up that it was clear they'd been designed for the dragons themselves to operate.

"I've got an idea," I said. "If Torcher gets inside, he might be able to make it go around."

"It's worth a try, Daniel," said Dr. Drake. He leaned down and whispered something to Torcher. In response, the dragon chick scrambled up the wall and along a thick rafter, then squirmed inside the wheel. He began walking doggedly forwards, and after a moment, the vast structure began to turn, causing a rumbling of the chains, which I now realised were attached to it. Gradually, another contraption rose into view. It was little more than a narrow beam, and I could not fathom its purpose.

"Come on!" Dr. Drake had already set off across the beam, balancing himself by spreading out his arms like a tightrope walker. Of course! It was a bridge. Knowing I had to cross it made the bridge seem narrower still. Beatrice glanced nervously towards me and back towards the beam, and we stood for a good few moments, wondering how best to approach it. Then came an angry roar behind us, and before we knew it, we had both sprinted across the bridge without a second thought. Torcher leapt down from the wheel and followed us across, scampering at our heels. I did not dare to look back. How on earth had the dragons managed to use it?

Almost the moment that we were across, Alexandra

Gorynytchka burst into the cavern, followed by two Tunguskas and a party of guards. The dragons' long necks were stretched out in front of them. It was as though they were sniffing their way forwards in the dark, despite the fact that their riders and the guards with them all carried bright torches. Dr. Drake released another lever on our side, which caused the bridge to trundle back down again and the wheel to disappear into its recess. Undaunted, the Tunguskas began to spread their wings, and I realised with horror that dragons did not need a bridge to cross the chasm. They could fly.

We fled onwards, but while the advancing Tunguskas blocked our way back, our way forward was also blocked — by a huge rockfall. Glancing around wildly, I spotted a supply of torches by a small opening at the far end of the cavern. "There!" I shouted.

We dived into a tunnel that was so low that Dr. Drake had to crawl on his hands and knees to get inside it. Still, at least we were safe from the Tunguskas, and as we progressed along the tunnel, it began to heighten, until even Torcher could stretch up on his hind legs without clipping his crest on the ceiling.

"Do you really think that this can lead to another way out?" asked Beatrice.

"If there is a way out, Torcher will find it," replied Dr. Drake calmly. He leaned across and whispered something in Dragonish in Torcher's ear, and the dragon chick sprinted ahead of us once more, lifting his head from time to time to sniff the air.

The passage soon led us into a much larger tunnel, which seemed to be the main thoroughfare Dr. Drake had spoken of. Following Torcher, we clambered through a chamber piled high with glittering treasure and hurried through an underground necropolis filled with rows of dragon tombs. Finally we reached a honeycomb network of round caves, the walls of which glinted with a thick, shimmering black substance.

"Look," exclaimed Dr. Drake. "Dragon dust. We must have reached the nesting caves."

"But there is so much of it," said Beatrice. "If Alexandra gets her hands on this, she'll be able to enslave dragons forever."

"It looks as if her men have already found it," said Dr. Drake, pointing out a pile of workman's tools in one corner.

Picking up a handful of the dust, I let it sift through my fingers and float to the ground. I looked up at Dr. Drake. "Maybe we should take some," I suggested.

"Good idea, Daniel," said Dr. Drake, stopping to gather some of the dust himself. "It may well come in handy."

We had only half filled our pockets, however, when we were thrown to the ground by yet another earth tremor, stronger than any that had gone before. I struggled to my feet and saw Torcher returning. He was racing towards us, followed by a terrific blast of hot air.

"Cover your mouths," Dr. Drake shouted, his voice hoarse and dry. "Try not to breathe in the gas."

The wave of air burned so strongly, it could have come from a blast furnace. I turned my face into my sleeve as it swept over me, and I emerged from it breathless and coughing, but otherwise unscathed. But on the other side of the cave, a glowing, fiery substance was slowly flowing towards us out of another tunnel.

"It's lava!" cried Beatrice. "Run!"

We sprinted away from the lava flow, following Torcher into a labyrinth of caves that had the appearance of individual dragon lairs. Though we escaped from the lava easily enough, the volcanic gases were now filling the tunnels of the lost city and making it harder and harder to breathe.

"Torcher, we've got to get out before we suffocate!" I cried, wishing that my Dragonish were better. He seemed to get the message, however, for moments later, he set off climbing diagonally up the cavern wall, as if it were the most natural thing in the world. Then he climbed across the cave roof and disappeared through a vent in the ceiling.

"H-how —?" I began.

"Look!" said Dr. Drake. He pointed to a series of thin ledges, like steps cut into the wall. "It's not as difficult as you might think."

"You mean, we've got to follow him up there?" asked Beatrice, incredulous.

"Don't worry, Bea," I said, trying to sound reassuring.

"I'll go first." I handed my torch to my sister and started to climb. All went well until I reached the top and realised I was stuck: to get to the vent I would have to swing hand over hand, like a monkey, across a row of bars that were fixed to the underside of the cave ceiling. I pondered for a moment, and realising I couldn't make it, I resolved to climb back down. But just at that moment, a liana vine tumbled out of the vent in the roof. It swayed backwards and forwards as if waiting for me to grab hold. Had Torcher thrown it down? Or was there someone else up there? There was no time for contemplation. Gingerly, I caught the vine and tugged on it hard, testing to see whether it would hold my weight.

"Torcher, is that you?" I called.

A familiar roar came in response, and so I took the vine in both hands and swung out under the hole, twisting my legs around it as I climbed upwards through the vent. I emerged into the moonlight and found Torcher with the vine between his teeth, his tail wound tightly around a convenient tree trunk.

"Good dragon!" I said, panting. I played the vine out down into the hole again, and a few minutes later Beatrice was at my side.

"Dr. Drake doesn't think he'll be able to climb up the wall," she said. "We'll have to find something to make the vine longer so that it can reach the floor."

"It's a good thing he didn't send us home, isn't it?" I said, knowing I was well out of Dr. Drake's earshot. I cast around and hauled another vine down from a tree and tied it to the first. Then I made a loop in the end and dropped it down through the vent. After a while I felt a tug, and Beatrice, Torcher, and I hauled up a smiling Dr. Drake. We were out at last! But where were we?

A short distance away, I could hear the familiar roar of a waterfall, and above us the sides of a gorge reached up steeply into the night sky.

"My goodness, we're back at the gorge, by the Cave of Dragons!" exclaimed Beatrice.

"Then we are not too far from the rune stone, are we?" said Dr. Drake. "Very well done, everyone. I am tremendously proud of you all." He patted Torcher on the back, and the young dragon looked extremely pleased with himself.

CHAPTER ELEVEN

THE RUNE STONE

That the Vikings discovered America is demonstrated by the Saga of Erik the Red, but denied by the pro-Columbus camp, who argue that there is a lack of archaeological evidence to match the literary record. That the Vikings discovered dragons —— and repeatedly attempted to pillage their hoards —— is, of course, beyond question.

—— *Dr. Ernest Drake, Letters to a Young Dragonologist*

W e were exhausted after the ordeal in the dragon city, but Beatrice and I agreed with Dr. Drake that it would be safer not to rest, but to get to the rune stone before daybreak. Once we arrived at the promontory, we pointed out the inscription on the stone, which Beatrice and I had been unable to read the first time we'd been here. Dr. Drake began studying it carefully.

"This is remarkable," he said after a few moments. With his finger, he traced the lines that marked out the image of a huge hammer. "These runes are written in Old Norse, one of the most ancient of the rune languages. Fortunately, I am well versed in it, as it is still used by some of the surviving dragons of northern Europe. Listen to what it says:

In the year of Christ 1012: Thorstan Longbeard —— a Viking, cousin to Leif the Lucky, finder of Vinland, and nephew to Erik the Red, discoverer of Greenland —— by the erection of this stone, lays claim to the place that he calls *Insula Draconis*, the Island of Dragons. Ten of his men were slain by the feathered fiends that dwell hereabouts. Thorstan swears that he shall return with a Viking army to conquer the land and slay the dragons, or drive them out forever. When the deed is done, the name Thorstan Longbeard shall be as famous in the sagas, for the discovery of the Isle of Dragons, as those of his uncle and cousin."

Beatrice was confused. "But I thought the dragons on this island were friendly towards humans?" she said.

Dr. Drake shook his head. "Not to those who wished to do them violence and steal their hoards." He was frowning intently at the stone. "But unfortunately, this text does not help us with Beatrice Croke's clue. The hammer we can see here isn't the Hammer of the Dragons, it is Mjölnir, the hammer of the Viking god Thor. The Vikings used it as a symbol even after most of them had converted to Christianity."

"What about the marks on the map?" I pointed to the outline of the island that Beatrice had discovered on the

other side of the stone. Now that I looked at them again, I realised that among the Norse runes were bits of Latin.

"Why didn't we see that before?" exclaimed Beatrice. "*Obeliscus, arena, mausoleo, pyramid.* The obelisk, arena, mausoleum, and pyramid are the places where Koa told us to look for clues. I can't quite make out the last inscription, though. *Hic sunt tres littera?*"

"Even I learned that much Latin at school," I said, pleased with myself. "It means 'here are three letters.' And look, there's another line of runes under the map," I said. "I don't know what they say, though."

"They aren't in Latin or Old Norse." Dr. Drake looked blank. "There's something funny about them. I'm not sure that I've ever seen an alphabet quite like that before. Most runic alphabets have letters with diagonal lines that slope down to the right, but these letters slope to the left."

"So they are the opposite way round?" I said. Suddenly an idea popped into my head. I tried it out, and to my delight, it worked. "I've got it!" I said. "They're dragon runes written backwards! And this time they are written in English."

"By Jove, you're right!" exclaimed Dr. Drake. "So come on, Daniel, tell us what they say."

And so I read out:

"*Dragon Master, choose with care,*
Grave danger waits for you.

Pick a place upon the map,
And there behold the clue.

RACOD-ACOR-RACODRA Arena
CORAD-ORAC-ODRACO Mausoleo
DRACO-RACO-ACODRAC Obeliscus
ODAC-ORRA-CODRACO Pyramid."

"But what does 'pick a place upon the map' mean?" said Beatrice.

I jumped in. "That's obvious. We have to choose a place on the map and go there to find the next clue."

Beatrice shook her head. "There's supposed to be a clue here, though. We have to look for three letters to go with the letter *A* that we have already found."

"What about the words in the second verse. They aren't in English, are they?" I said. "I've only ever heard of DRACO-RACO-ACODRAC. Dr. Drake, wasn't that the password you used to claim the Dragon's Eye?"

"Indeed it is," Dr. Drake confirmed. "What a fine memory you have."

"But choosing that word would mean we should go to the obelisk," said Beatrice. "We're already at the obelisk. So where's the clue?"

I scratched my fingernail over the surface of the map. "It doesn't say that we have to go to the obelisk," I said. "It says we must 'pick a place upon a map.' If you look closely, the runes are on a different background from the rest of the map. Look, it seems to be a sort of plaster. Perhaps you can just pick them off."

I began levering out a nail under the runes that spelled out *arena*. Carefully, I picked away at the plaster, until I could feel something behind it, trying to force its way out. I leapt back with a shout of terror as a barbed arrow flew out of the hole, a bead of purple liquid shining on its silver tip.

"What on earth are you doing, Daniel!" exclaimed Beatrice. Her face was white, and I've no doubt mine was, too.

"I'm sorry," I said. I was mortified. "I didn't think for a moment that there would be anything behind there."

"You didn't think at all, Daniel," said Dr. Drake sternly. "The warning about grave danger should have at least alerted you to the possibility of fatal booby traps. Your insatiable curiosity is going to be the death of you one of these days, young man."

"I'm sorry," I said, bowing my head humbly. My hands were still shaking from the shock. I tried to calm myself and gather my wits about me again. "But what do you suggest we do?" I asked.

Beatrice thought for a moment. "Pick away the right letters, of course. The obelisk."

"You had better let me do it this time!" said Dr. Drake curtly.

Dr. Drake picked at the plaster much more carefully

than I had done. At last, it fell away to reveal a round hole, from which he pulled a thin tube of beaten gold. Inside was a second draccum scroll. Dr. Drake unfurled the parchment carefully and read out the clue. It was written in plain — if old-fashioned — English.

> *"To my eminent and esteemed successor. Know this: the Hammer of the Dragons, carved from a stone that fell from the sky, cannot do its work without its partner, an anvil, formed from a rare crystal. Never allow the one to strike the other in the presence of dragons, for the far-carrying sound thus produced initiates a perilous vibration deep within their bodies. This vibration disrupts the regular palpitations of their hearts, quickening them until they burst and are consumed from within by the corrosive action of their own blood. And therein lies the awful power of the hammer. Do not tarry, but hasten to the next clue.*
>
> *Go with dragon speed!*
>
> *Beatrice Croke."*

Dr. Drake scowled. "Of all the infernal devices ever created by man for the destruction of his fellow creatures, I must say that this is one of the very worst."

"It's disgusting." Beatrice cast a worried glance at

Torcher, who was sitting a short distance away on the cliff top. "Can it really do that?"

Dr. Drake stroked his moustache for a moment. "Yes, I believe that it could. You and Daniel will have learned about the corrosive properties of dragon's blood in your dragonology lessons, but what you do not know, perhaps, is that a dragon's hard, scaly skin makes it unusually sensitive to sound vibrations. Coupled with the fact that their hearts have six chambers, while ours have merely four . . ."

"But how can a sound cause their hearts to explode?" Beatrice looked sceptical.

"Have you ever seen the trick where an opera singer causes a crystal glass to shatter by the vibration of a particularly high note she sings?"

We both nodded and I made a face. "I thought my eardrums were going to burst."

"It may be something similar to that. Having six chambers, the dragon's heart is very delicately balanced, and it is susceptible to irregular palpitations. The heartbeat overcompensates for those palpitations by speeding up." Dr. Drake shook his head and reread the scroll to himself. "However did Dobrinja discover such a terrible thing? These noble creatures pay a high price for their many evolutionary advantages."

"Well, the sooner the hammer is destroyed the better,"

said Beatrice as if suddenly resolving herself to action. "Right, what is the next clue?"

Dr. Drake turned back to the parchment. "Like Beatrice Croke's last message, there is both a clue and a verse that tells us where to look next. But this time the clue simply has two lines:

> *Using a dragon's eye,*
> *Three letters you shall spy.*

The rhyme then follows:

> *Here lie two English lords, in life*
> *The causes of a kingdom's strife.*
> *Their wicked wars were all in vain,*
> *At last by vengeful dragons slain."*

Dr. Drake held up the draccum and peered at it through the lens of the Dragon's Eye. Then he turned it over and looked at the other side with a perplexed expression.

"I cannot see any letters here," he said.

"Maybe they have faded," I suggested.

Dr. Drake shook his head, as he handed the draccum and the Dragon's Eye to Beatrice. "Letters inscribed on draccum do not fade."

"But there's absolutely nothing here," she exclaimed

as she studied the parchment through the gem. "We have come this far. The letters must be there!" She thought for a moment. "What if they're concealed on the paper in some other way?"

Beatrice ran her fingers over the parchment, but I shook my head.

"The message is pretty clear," I said. "'Use a dragon's eye.'"

"Of course!" said Beatrice. "We don't need the Dragon's Eye—we need a dragon's eye. Torcher, come here, boy!'

"Beatrice, you're a marvel!" I said. "But we'll never get Torcher to tell us what the letters are."

"Oh, no?" said Beatrice. "I've got an idea." Torcher had scampered over to her and was sitting eagerly at her side, proud to be of service. She pointed to one of the rune letters on the stone and traced it with her finger in the dirt. After that, she held Torcher's foreclaw and used it to gently trace out the same letter. Then, she showed him the parchment. He studied it for a moment and then carefully drew three letters with his foreclaw: *D, E,* and *N.*

"Den!" exclaimed Dr. Drake. "Well done, Torcher!"

"So now we have four letters," I said. "And from the sound of the verse, it seems clear that next we need to go to the mausoleum where Beatrice buried the Dragonsbane Knights."

"But the map says it's on the other side of the volcano,"

said Beatrice. "How are we going to get there without being seen?"

I reached into my pocket and pulled out a handful of dragon dust. I'd been thinking about it ever since I'd suggested we take some with us. I'd been trying to remember a spell that I was sure could come in useful. "We're just going to have to catch a Tunguska!" I said blythly.

Beatrice's face fell. "This is no time for jokes, Daniel."

"Actually, I'm not joking," I said. "Don't you remember Abramelin's Taming Spell?"

The spell had required casting three troy ounces of dragon dust over a dragon from a silver dish that had been washed three times in water that had reflected a full moon. As the dust was cast, the user needed to recite a special charm. Beatrice and I had used the spell on Idraigir, after he had been charmed by Ignatius Crook. Even though we had been unsure about the quantities of dust, it had worked well.

"I think I can remember the words," said Beatrice. "But don't we need a silver dish?"

"Let's look in Koa's hoard," I suggested. "A silver dish is exactly the sort of thing you would expect to find there. It's bound to have been washed more than three times, and all water has reflected a full moon at one time, hasn't it?"

"Good thinking, Daniel," said Dr. Drake. "We are certainly in urgent need of food and rest. Let us go to Koa's cave. I'm sure that we will soon find a way out of our predicament."

CHAPTER TWELVE

THE JUNGLE TOMB

I have never considered myself a coward, but I would far
rather face a thousand fire-breathing dragons on a jungle
trek than fifty hungry mosquitoes.

—— *Dr. Ernest Drake, Letters to a Young Dragonologist*

Koa had left plentiful supplies in his cave, and a few
hours later, the sun was high in the sky and we felt
rested enough to continue with the quest. Beatrice found
several silver dishes in Koa's hoard, but she still looked
doubtful.

"Do you think Abramelin's Taming Spell will really
work with one of these?" she said, turning a small, battered-
looking dish over in her hand. "Because we're going to be
in a nasty spot if it doesn't. And how are we going to get a
Tunguska to come near enough for it to work?"

"Abramelin's spell has never been known to fail if you
have enough dragon dust," said Dr. Drake. "And as for
attracting a Tunguska, that shouldn't be a problem. The tide
is out; a little stroll along the shore ought to do the trick."

A short while later Dr. Drake set out along the beach, while Beatrice, Torcher, and I stayed hidden behind a few large rocks. Just as Dr. Drake had predicted, it wasn't long before a Tunguska spotted him and swooped towards him eagerly. I bit my lip. What if Alexandra's orders had changed? What if she had found the Hammer of the Dragons and no longer needed to keep us alive? I needn't have worried. Everything went according to plan. Torcher sprang from his hiding place, sank his teeth into the Tunguska's tail, and scampered out of range before the Tunguska could attempt to incinerate him. Meanwhile, Beatrice and I stepped out from behind the rocks on the creature's other side and showered it with handfuls of dragon dust while uttering the words of the spell we had last used far away on the slopes of Ben Wyvis:

> "Ivàhsi yüduin!
> Enimôr taym inspelz!
> Boyar ugôner gedit!"

There was a frightening moment when it seemed as though the spell hadn't worked and the Tunguska was going to snap our heads off, but then it appeared to freeze, and a dazed expression came over its face.

"Look over here," ordered Beatrice. The Tunguska obeyed, turning its head towards her. "Sit down," she commanded. It obeyed again.

"So you understand some English, at least," she continued. "That is good. Now, there is an old building on the other side of this island. It is a mausoleum. I want you to take us there."

The Tunguska looked blank.

"How should I say 'mausoleum' in Dragonish?" Beatrice asked Dr. Drake.

"You could try *hoyar-gretch-loc*. Dragons sometimes use that to refer to human cemeteries. It means 'man-death-place,' but I think that simple commands will be the most efficacious in this instance. It has probably never seen the mausoleum, but you can always try."

We climbed up onto the Tunguska's back.

"*Algroo hoyar-gretch-loc!*" commanded Beatrice. "*Algroo hoyar-gretch-loc.*"

But the dragon did not understand Beatrice, for it remained seated with the same blank expression on its face.

"Maybe I should just ask it to take off?" she said, thinking aloud.

"Then you'll need to say *gerupthar,*" I told her. "And, don't forget, *drexx* means 'right' and *nisster* means 'left.'" I was pleased with myself for remembering the words, but Beatrice shot me an irritated look. Of course, she wasn't asking me. Her Dragonish was far better than mine.

The Tunguska responded well to the simpler commands and quickly took off, flying exactly as Beatrice directed. I was greatly relieved, for I had felt most uncomfortable sitting astride an uncooperative enemy dragon, tamed or not, especially as we did not know how temporary the effects of the spell might be. The Tunguska flew us in a wide arc that took us far out over the sea and back towards the island on the other side. Several times we flew over the area of jungle where we knew the mausoleum should be, but the dense canopy of trees made it impossible to spot anything on the ground except for a river that snaked towards the sea.

"Do you remember those wavy lines on the map?" I ventured.

"You mean, the ones that look like rivers?" asked Dr. Drake.

"Yes. I'm sure the mausoleum was next to one of them."

"You're right, Daniel!" Dr. Drake exclaimed, turning to Beatrice, who still had firm command of the Tunguska. "Tell the dragon to set us down somewhere near the mouth of this river."

A few minutes later we were standing on a beach of white sand. We looked around cautiously to check that we had not been seen, but Torcher seemed jumpy and ill at ease.

"Something's making Torcher anxious," called Beatrice.

"I'm anxious, too," said Dr. Drake, pointing out several Tunguskas that had just appeared above the flank of the volcano. "They haven't seen us yet. But I think it is time that we let this dragon go. It cannot help us in the jungle."

Beatrice instructed the Tunguska to forget our

encounter, and she sent it on its way. As it flew up to join its fellow dragons, we hurried off the beach towards the cover of some palm trees.

"Now, let us make haste before a search party finds us," said Dr. Drake.

It was easier said than done, for the river did not have any well-defined banks. Trees and tangled shrubs grew out of the shallows at the edge, so that we had to follow the flow of the water from a distance. Finally, when I was convinced that we were fighting our way up the wrong river, Torcher, for whom neither the undergrowth nor the biting flies proved any obstacle, took hold of my sleeve and began pulling me onwards. He let go of me in front of a tree that, to my surprise and relief, had a dragon's skull carved on its trunk and an arrow pointing to the left.

"We're getting close," I called to the others. The jungle was so dense that it was impossible to see more than a few feet ahead, but a short distance farther on, Beatrice let out a cry. "There it is!"

The mausoleum was a small rectangular building set in a clearing. It had a wooden door and the names "Norfolk" and "Northumberland" carved on a stone lintel. The names of the two Dragonsbane Knights.

"They were a long way from home," said Beatrice. "What brought them here?"

"They were banished from England by King Edward,"

said Dr. Drake. "Whenever they slew a dragon, they were supposed to divide up a third of the treasure between themselves and give the rest to the king. Edward claimed that although they had given him his due in gold and jewels, they had kept several particularly valuable pieces for themselves. Among these were many of the items that we now recognise as the twelve treasures of the S.A.S.D. King Edward also feared that the Dragonsbane Knights were secretly planning to stop slaying dragons and use the treasures to form a dragon army against him. He believed that they aimed to topple him and claim the crown of England for themselves. From that moment on it became a crime even to speak of Dragonsbane."

"Did they really want to depose him?" I asked.

Dr. Drake nodded. "Quite possibly. At first King Edward had kept the hammer for his own protection, in case he should ever be attacked by a dragon. He only let the Dragonsbane Knights have it later, when they had already slain several powerful dragons. However, the knights didn't use it, and I believe this roused the king's suspicion that they might be planning to enslave rather than kill dragons in the future. And the only reason for that, which he could see, was that they wanted to take his throne."

"It seems odd that Beatrice Croke built a mausoleum for her enemies, though," Beatrice commented.

"But to all intents and purposes, Beatrice Croke was a

knight herself," Dr. Drake explained. "She believed in chivalry and generosity and all of the other knightly virtues. And, in any case, I suppose she needed somewhere to put the third clue that would remind people of the danger posed by Dragonsbane. What better place than the tomb of its vanquished leaders?"

I tried the door, but it did not move. There was a small plaque by the handle with an inscription on it:

> *Here lie two English lords, in life*
> *The causes of a kingdom's strife.*
> *Their wicked wars were all in vain,*
> *At last by vengeful dragons slain.*
>
> *In silent death, being interred,*
> *These fallen knights now guard a word.*
> *A lick of flame shall let you in*
> *From one that wears a dragon's skin.*
>
> *The clue you seek is hidden here,*
> *But for the wise the way is clear:*
> *The time to knock is not before,*
> *But after opening up the door.*

"'A lick of flame shall let you in,'" I said, slowly realising the meaning of the second verse. But as usual, Beatrice got to the answer much faster than I did.

"Come on, Torcher!" she said. "It's time to do your bit again."

Torcher breathed fire on the lock of the mausoleum, and the door swung open to reveal a plain chamber that contained two stone tombs.

"What do we do now?" I said. "The rhyme says something about knocking after we open the door."

"Yes, but knock where?" said Dr. Drake. "On the tombs?" He rapped on the top of one of them, but his hand hardly made a sound against the heavy stone lid.

"Ugh," said Beatrice with a shudder. "I hope we're not going to find the clue clutched in the hand of a skeleton."

"That is a possibility, Beatrice," said Dr. Drake. "Let's try to move the lids."

I stood on one side of the tomb while Beatrice stomped around to the other side. "Wait a moment," she said. She banged her foot, and a hollow sound rang out. "There may be something under here."

Dr. Drake knocked on the floor in the same place and got the same result.

"The clue must be underneath the flagstones," he said.

I helped Dr. Drake heave up one of the heavy slabs. We were in luck. Underneath was a shallow pit that contained a dragon-skin bag and a third draccum parchment. He unrolled it to reveal a paragraph in Beatrice Croke's handwriting on one side and a riddle on the other. The riddle read:

Two letters here let seekers seek,
Not for the cautious, or the weak.
Be bold, and let rough action start:
Rip off a head, tear out a heart.
Hardrada had an amulet;
And so, my kin, do not forget.

"Ugh, that's disgusting!" Beatrice looked at the tombs in distaste.

"Don't worry, Bea," I said. "I'm sure we won't have to dissect any corpses." I couldn't understand why she felt so squeamish all of a sudden. "But Beatrice Croke didn't expect us to bring the treasures of the S.A.S.D. here, did she? 'Hardrada had an amulet' must refer to Splatterfax, the amulet of the Viking Rus. But it doesn't have a head."

"If it's a riddle, like the others, you mustn't take it too literally," answered my sister.

"Yes, but what does she mean by 'kin'?" I mused.

"Her kin must mean her family," said Beatrice. "But who could be the heart of her family?"

"Her family was the Crokes," I said. "They were our ancestors, so they're our family, too."

"I shouldn't think that's important," said Dr. Drake. "We have to think about it in terms of the letters. So the head of Splatterfax —"

"— is the letter *S*," Beatrice interrupted him excitedly.

"And her family name is Croke. And at the 'heart' of Croke is the letter *O*."

"Brilliant!" I exclaimed. "Which means that, so far, we've got A DEN SO."

"Yes, but 'a den so . . .' what? Big? Small? It doesn't make any sense," replied Beatrice. "And I really don't see how it is going to lead us to a key."

"Unless the answer is a riddle itself," I suggested.

"A riddle that leads to another riddle?" said Beatrice, sounding only slightly exasperated. "Now, that would be dragonological."

"I'm afraid we're going to have to uncover the final clue to find out," said Dr. Drake.

"There's only the pyramid left now," I said, suddenly feeling that we had a chance of succeeding.

"But we need to see what the parchment says, first," Beatrice reminded us.

Dr. Drake dutifully unfurled the draccum and read out our ancestor's message:

"To my esteemed successor. Congratulations! The hour of the prophecy draws nigh, and were I still alive it would be heartening to know that the teaching of the Dragon Masters has not yet faltered.

In these tombs lie the last two lords of Dragonsbane. After wickedly unleashing the terrible power of Dobrinja's hammer upon this island, slaying all of the dragon inhabitants, they were justly slain by the vengeful amphithere Koa and his brother, Kua.

Vim promovet draconis. *Your final clue lies close.*

Go with dragon speed,

Beatrice Croke

> *On Aztec steps hide four last letters,*
> *To free a hammer from its fetters!*
> *Look above to solve this clue,*
> *Then watch the master watching you!"*

CHAPTER THIRTEEN

THE DRAGON VINE

For a class of animals that is, in the main, solitary, the amount of
gossip spread between one dragon and the next —— even if they live
hundreds of miles distant —— is nothing less than remarkable.

—— *Dr. Ernest Drake, Letters to a Young Dragonologist*

W e could not traverse the impenetrable jungle, so the
only way to reach the northern part of the island —
without trying to attract another Tunguska — was to go
around the coast. We made slow progress and it was nearly
dark when Torcher, who had been exploring up ahead,
came running back in a state of great excitement.

"What is it, old fellow?" I asked.

Dr. Drake pointed to a distant dot above the sea. "Look!"

"Is it a dragon?" asked Beatrice.

"It is three dragons, if you please," said Dr. Drake with
a relieved grin. Then, to my amazement, he began running along the beach, waving his arms wildly. *"Praisich!
Praisich!"* he shouted, using the Dragonish word for 'hello.'
"Over here!"

"It's Koa!" cried Beatrice. "But who are the dragons he's brought with him?"

"I don't believe it!" I shouted. "It's Idraigir!"

"And Erasmus!" yelled Beatrice. "I never thought I'd see him again." Now all three of us were running along the beach, waving our arms, desperate to attract their attention.

They saw us, and we moved aside swiftly, as the three majestic creatures flew in to land on the beach beside us. We ran to greet them, and Beatrice flung her arms around Erasmus, who looked strangely bashful.

"Do you know what happened to our parents?" she asked with a concerned frown.

It was Idraigir who answered. "They are safe," he said. "I have sent word to them that you are the ones of whom the prophecy speaks."

"You know about the prophecy?" I was surprised and relieved, if a little irritated that Idraigir had known about the prophecy all along. But there were more important questions to consider just now. "How did our parents escape?" I asked.

"You were right to guess that your parents had spotted Tingi," said Erasmus. "When the Tunguskas attacked the hunting lodge and set fire to it, your parents were searching for him, as you had suggested. They took shelter in a cellar in the garden."

"What, in the old icehouse?" exclaimed Beatrice.

"Yes. They were safe there, but they had a difficult

time explaining to the police why they thought the hunting lodge had burned down — and why Eilean Donan Castle had suddenly become even more ruinous — without mentioning dragons! They decided that discretion was the better part of valour, and I helped them to leave before they were arrested. I took them to Wharncliffe to consult with Idraigir, and there we agreed that Idraigir and I should do our best to pick up your trail, while your parents went to London to arrange a rescue expedition. They are staying with Mr. Tibbs."

"That must be delightful for them," said Beatrice dryly, remembering the disagreeable little man from S.A.S.D. headquarters. "But what happened to you and Tingi?"

Erasmus hung his head. "I fought long and hard against the Tunguskas, but in the end my strength was overcome."

"We feared you had been killed," I said. "I saw you fall into the loch."

"I was forced to make a hard choice. To die fighting — the nobler way — or to flee in shame. One dragon had to live to carry word to Idraigir of what had happened."

"What about Tingi?" I asked.

"Tingi the brave will not be returning to the lands of the midnight sun," said Erasmus. "He fought to the bitter end, and now his cave will lie cold and empty."

We were all silent and Dr. Drake bowed his head.

"He was a great and noble dragon," Erasmus said solemnly. "Loyal to his kinsfolk and faithful to his people. It was an honour to be able to call him my brother. He will not be forgotten."

"Indeed he will not," responded Idraigir. "He was a great and noble friend."

Now that we had paid our respects to Tingi, something was worrying me. Idraigir, Koa, and Erasmus were mighty dragons, but they were only three against an army of thousands.

"Are there more dragons coming?" I asked.

"They are mustering in the high Atlas Mountains," said Idraigir. "News has spread quickly via the Dragon Vine; many of us have waited a long time in anticipation of this day, and now Koa tells us that the time of the prophecy is finally at hand."

"But how did you know about the prophecy?" I asked.

Idraigir raised his head a little haughtily. "We dragons have known about it for centuries," he replied. "The details of it are written in *Liber Draconis*."

"*Liber Draconis*?" Dr. Drake was taken aback. "I have not seen it mentioned there."

"That is because you have applied the fire of only three species of dragons to its pages," replied Idraigir. "A European dragon, a wyvern, and a *lung*. Thus, you have read only the parts that are relevant to those species."

Koa stepped forwards. "Idraigir speaks the truth. To read the prophecy, you must apply a fourth fire: the flame of an amphithere."

I was confused. "But I thought that *Liber Draconis* was a diary. . . ."

"And so it is. The greatest—possibly the only—diary to have been written by a dragon this side of the Tien Shan Mountains." Koa looked out to sea. "Come," he said. "The night will not last forever. I think it will be better if we speak of such things in the safety of my cave. On the way, I will show you the forces arrayed against us, but you must remain silent, for now is not the time to draw out our enemy."

As we mounted the dragons—Beatrice and I riding on Erasmus—I felt a wave of exhaustion wash over me. It was a relief that we no longer had to walk to the pyramid. Soon we were flying over a wide desert plain that was strewn with numerous vast black boulders. There were so many of them, I began to wonder about them, and then a shiver ran down my spine. These were not boulders at all, but instead thousands upon thousands of slumbering dragons: Alexandra Gorynytchka's army.

Beatrice looked horrified. "Now I know why she needs so much dragon dust." She grimaced. "But how does she feed so many?"

Erasmus spat out, "Bison, buffalo, whale—whatever her foraging dragons can find. She has supplies flown in each day."

"And where does she get the men to control such a vast army?" I quizzed.

"From Siberia and Tunguska, mainly," Erasmus

answered, the disgust still apparent in his tone. "She has agents all over the world."

Beatrice shook her head. "But surely Alexandra's army is simply too powerful," she said. "Even if we find the hammer, how is Dr. Drake going to save so many dragons?"

"We must trust in the prophecy," said Erasmus quietly.

Once at the cave, there was little time to rest. No sooner had we entered than Koa thrust a large golden box into my arms. It was engraved with the head of a bull. "Open it," he told me.

Inside was a green leather-bound book, its cover embossed with a picture of a dragon curled around a book. I opened it and read the title in wonder. *"Liber Draconis."*

"But it can't be," said Beatrice, rushing to my side to see for herself. *"Liber Draconis* is in Wyvern Way."

"There are two copies," said Koa. "You hold in your hands the original book. Medieval Dragon Master Gildas Magnus made a copy to be kept safe by the Dragon Masters. It was gradually added to after his lifetime."

"But I thought the original was kept in Spain," said Beatrice.

"And so it was for many years," Koa confirmed, "for the book's author had many human friends there. But he returned it to me before he died, with a warning that the time of the prophecy was at hand."

"You know who wrote it?" gasped Beatrice. "Who was he?"

"One I knew very well," said Koa mysteriously. "He was my brother, Kua."

"Kua!" exclaimed Dr. Drake. "It was he who wrote *Liber Draconis*?"

Koa inclined his head. "It was his dream that the achievements of the dragons of Atlantis might be rekindled. He imagined a new group of dragon scholars studying humanology in the future, so that the two species might be brought closer together. At Beatrice Croke's behest, he included information in the book about the prophecy and established the Dragon Vine and the Dragon Express. While I agreed to guard the Hammer of the Dragons here, he set out to discover what he could about the coming evil. Alas! He died of the dragon plague, contained in a vial of powder that was taken from this island by Gildas Magnus."

"But how did Kua come to be infected with the powder?" asked Dr. Drake. "Alexandra Gorynytchka opened the vial only a few years ago."

"My brother's death was very recent. He was attempting to rescue a dragon chick that Alexandra had poisoned during her early experiments with the powder, before its true properties were known."

"Scorcher!" Beatrice and I said at the same time, remembering Torcher's older brother.

"I believe that was his name," said Koa dismissively. "Now, place *Liber Draconis* on the floor, open the middle pages, and stand back."

Koa blew a jet of multicoloured flame over the book, and instantly the pages sprang to life. Dr. Drake leaned forwards eagerly to examine the elaborate script. Then he picked up the book and read:

"Here follows the terrible tale of Dobrinja's hammer: Many years ago, in the kingdom of Rus, there lived a proud king called Yaroslav who dreamed of enlarging his kingdom to the east and to the west. To expand westwards posed few problems. He hired mercenary Vikings to fight for him, and he quickly acquired new lands. His expansion eastwards, however, was far more difficult, for the residents of the eastern lands were a fierce and terrifying foe who would fight boldly to defend their territory. The eastern lands were home, of course, to a great number of dragons.

So, instead of sending armies to the east, King Yaroslav sent out his spies. They soon came across a shaman named Dobrinja who lived among the dragons and was a friend to them. As part of his craft, however, Dobrinja had created many wonderous objects that could be used to control and temper the dragons. In fact, he had grown overbold, for in his pride he had forged a certain hammer from a block of sky-stone, with an anvil of rare crystal to match it. When these were struck together, this hammer and anvil were capable of slaying any dragons within earshot at a single stroke.

Dobrinja intended the hammer to be used purely as a

defensive weapon, but alas, one day, its power was unleashed in a moment of recklessness. Dobrinja's best friend was a dragon, and while most times they enjoyed each other's company, the dragon and the shaman argued bitterly over the hammer and the anvil. While Dobrinja maintained that the hammer would serve dragons well, his dragon friend believed that no good would come of it, and he begged Dobrinja to destroy it. The pair fell into a bitter argument, and in a fit of rage, Dobrinja struck the hammer on the anvil, killing the best friend instantly.

Seeing his friend's heart burst, and his black blood consume him, Dobrinja bitterly rued the day he had created the weapon, and he understood that his friend had been right all along. Straightaway, he began to plan how he might destroy the hammer.

Meanwhile, King Yaroslav's spies had witnessed the power of the hammer, and they set about persuading Dobrinja to preserve it. They told him that King Yaroslav's daughter had been kidnapped by a dragon who was demanding a ransom of three children per week for her return. They begged Dobrinja to accompany them with his dreadful weapon, in order to save the princess.

Reluctantly, Dobrinja agreed. On reaching Kiev, however, Dobrinja learned that he had been tricked. The hammer was taken from him and given into the stewardship of a warrior named Ivan Gorynytch, to keep until the king's armies were ready to march eastwards. For the hammer was the answer to King Yaroslav's dream: it would slay all the dragons his men encountered, so that the king could expand his kingdom to the east.

After many failed attempts to retrieve the hammer, Dobrinja, full of remorse for having created such a baleful weapon, flung himself into the Dnieper River, uttering the words of the prophecy as the icy waters carried him away."

Dr. Drake looked up from the page and Beatrice frowned. "Do you think Ivan Gorynytch is any relation to Alexandra Gorynytchka?" she asked.

"Indeed, he is her ancestor," Koa answered. "But he did not keep the hammer for long. King Yaroslav lent it to a Viking warrior named Harald Hardrada, who failed to return it. When the hammer was taken from him, Gorynytch swore a terrible oath that he or his heirs would one day regain it."

"So that's what Alexandra is trying to do!" I exclaimed. "She wants to regain the hammer because of an oath made by her ancestor."

"That, or get revenge on dragonkind for the slaying of her entire family by a party of Tunguskas," said Dr. Drake.

There was silence for a moment, until Beatrice spoke up. "Do we know the actual words of the prophecy?"

"Turn the page and you will see them," said Koa,

pointing to *Liber Draconis*. "The original prophecy is in medieval Russian, but Kua has placed a translation beneath:

I curse the dark day the terrible hammer was made,
The greatest evil ever that dragons shall have to face,
Until an evil to match that matchless evil shall rise,
Only then can the hammer be broken, flung in a fiery pit.

An army of dragons shall fly to fight against dragons enslaved,
An army of cruel men, and standing against them but three,
A dragon master, and two not yet full grown,
Wise in the ways of dragons and brave beyond their years.

Against such terrible evils, a sacrifice shall be made;
In a noble dragon's death lies the dragons' hope.
At the moment of its triumph, evil will be betrayed,
Then the evil shall die, and the dragons shall all be free."

CHAPTER FOURTEEN
THE PYRAMID

O! The sights I have seen and the places I have been. And all with
but a single goal: the conservation and preservation of dragons.
—— *Dr. Ernest Drake, Letters to a Young Dragonologist*

After the conference in the cave, we rested, and we
awoke before dawn. Koa informed us that finding
the final clue would be our most difficult test yet, for the
pyramid lay in a complex of heavily guarded ruins that were
at the very centre of Alexandra's operations on the island.
The dragons were depending on us; we could not afford
to fail.

Erasmus and Idraigir flew on ahead to try to draw away
any search parties of Tunguskas patrolling the skies. Then
Koa flew us to the misty northern part of the island, where
an Aztec pyramid rose above a thick forest of palms. Koa set
the four of us down in a damp gully hidden among the trees,
but still near to the high wall that surrounded the pyramid

complex. There was a single entrance in the wall, a stone gateway; my heart sank when I saw that it was guarded by a pair of dozing Tunguskas and two heavily armed men.

Suddenly, the Tunguskas stirred, and one of the men began speaking to the other in an agitated voice, grabbing his shoulder and pointing. I held my breath, for I was sure he must have seen us, but it seemed he was gesturing at something over our heads. Far away a jet of black smoke was surging from the top of the volcano, and I had an uneasy feeling that all was not going according to plan. "Where's Torcher?" I gasped, realising that the dragon chick was no longer at our side. I let out a sigh of relief when I spotted the movement of his scales giving him away as he crept through the undergrowth towards the gate.

"What does he think he's doing?" I hissed.

Dr. Drake was watching him like a hawk. "My guess is that he plans to copy Idraigir and provide us with a distraction."

"He's too small! They'll catch him." Beatrice lurched forwards, but Dr. Drake put out a hand to hold her back.

"Please, Beatrice," he whispered. "You must have faith in Torcher. We are putting our own lives in danger as well, remember."

I did not move a muscle as Torcher crept up on the larger of the two Tunguskas and plunged his teeth into its tail. The dragon let out an anguished roar and spun around just in time to spot Torcher scampering away. Roaring again, this time with fierce rage, he poured out a jet of flame that set the nearest trees on fire. Then, both dragons plunged after Torcher into the burning jungle, and following a moment of confusion, the guards began to chase them, too, uttering loud oaths as they dodged around the outer edge of the forest fire.

"It's now or never," said Dr. Drake.

He sprinted across the patch of open ground in front of the gateway. We followed him inside. The pyramid fronted the far side of a huge square that was surrounded by buildings in various states of ruinous decay. There did not seem to be anyone about, but Dr. Drake quickly ducked behind the first ruined building and then in at the door of another, much larger one, which appeared to be more or less intact. Its rooms had been furnished with opulent-looking rugs and dark wood chairs, and as my eyes adjusted to the darkness, I could even make out crystal chandeliers suspended from the ceiling. "So this is Alexandra's hideout," I said. It felt decidedly creepy.

"Unfortunately, we don't have any time for sightseeing," replied Dr. Drake. "But I'll wager that if we take this corridor it will bring us out nearer to the pyramid. Hopefully unobserved."

We set off and soon came to what appeared to be a throne room. Behind the throne—a gilded monstrosity that looked like a dragon's gaping maw—was a smaller chamber, protected by stout bars. Although we were in a hurry,

I could not help peering inside, and I gasped at what I saw. Along with a hoard of gold and silver, there were several objects that I instantly recognised: Splatterfax, the Spear of Saint George, and three red-bound books that I recognised straightaway as those that Ignatius Crook had stolen from Castle Drake during the search for the Dragon's Eye.

"It's your dragon diaries!" I exclaimed to Dr. Drake.

But even as he hastened to my side, the sound of voices came from outside. Dr. Drake let his eyes rest on his precious dragonological record books for an instant, then turned away. "Come," he said. "We mustn't let them catch us."

There was a window in a small room farther along the corridor, and we climbed out into a narrow alley. One end of it led out onto the large square, and we found ourselves in front of the pyramid. On each of its wide steps, carvings depicted dragons engaged in a variety of horrible activities: piling up human skulls, burning human bodies, and feeding human arms and legs to their hungry chicks. I shuddered at the sight of them.

"Do we really have to go up there?" asked Beatrice.

"We have to get right to the top," said Dr. Drake. "It is the most likely place, don't you think? The rhyme said, 'Look above to solve this clue,' remember?"

There were no guards visible, but every muscle felt tense as we crossed the open square and hastened up the steps. At the top was a small building, empty apart from an ornate circular table that lay directly beneath a hole of similar dimensions in the ceiling. The table was painted with a frieze that showed various animals and birds. And in the very centre, baring sharp fangs, as though master of them all, was a dragon.

"Why is it sticking out its tongue?" exclaimed Beatrice.

"That's not a tongue," said Dr. Drake. "It is a heart that the dragon is devouring."

Beatrice looked pale. "What is this place?"

"This is a sacrificial pyramid." Dr. Drake let his hand hover above the table. "And here is the altar where the priests cut out the hearts of their human victims. The Aztec people worshipped the dragons here, believing them to be gods."

"Look." I pointed to where guards were running across the plaza below. "They must have seen us. Where do we look for the clue?"

"What about the letters on the table?" suggested Beatrice, her eyes scanning the painting.

"What letters?" Even Dr. Drake seemed mystified.

Beatrice pointed to one of the pictures around the edge of the table. "Look there."

"It's a snake," I said.

"Not the snake, look next to it." I screwed up my eyes, stared hard, and sure enough, there, carved with the faintest of marks, was a rune symbol—an *E*. There were tiny rune marks next to all of the pictures around the table: a dragon marked *F;* a flower *U;* a jaguar *TH;* a warrior *A;* a drinking

cup *R;* a dagger *K;* a skull *G;* an eagle *Y;* a snake *E;* and many more that I did not have time to study.

"Can you make sense of it?" I asked Dr. Drake. Outside, the guards had reached the base of the pyramid and were fanning out around it.

"It's a runic picture alphabet," he said. "The runes tell us which letter each picture represents. But we are looking for only four letters, and there are many more than that here."

"There are two more rune marks on the heart in the dragon's mouth." I said. "*U* and *P*—up."

For a moment, Beatrice looked puzzled. Then she tilted her head back and scoured the ceiling. "Perhaps 'up' is where we have to look for the clues."

Above us, the ceiling was plain and, but for the hole, bare of any decoration. "There's nothing there," I said.

Suddenly, a shout from outside made us freeze. One of the guards was pointing in our direction, and an all-too-familiar creature was zigzagging its way across the plaza.

"Flitz!" Beatrice cried. That was the last thing we needed. And now the guards had started to mount the steps.

"What about the roof?" I said. "That's up, isn't it? And from there I can use my dragon whistle to call for help."

Quickly, we climbed onto the sacrificial table, then scrambled through the hole in the ceiling and onto the flat roof. I blew my dragon whistle, but the skies remained empty. The roof was bare except for four stone blocks that must have been left over when the pyramid was built. Meanwhile the guards were getting closer.

"Perhaps we could throw these at them," I said, picking up one of the stones.

"Stop, Daniel!" exclaimed Beatrice. "Look, there's a picture on it!"

I turned the stone over in my hand. "Goodness, you're right. It's a skull!"

Beatrice bent to pick up another one and found a picture of a drinking cup. "Maybe the pictures on these stones tell us the four final letters. According to the runes on the altar, the skull represents the letter *G* and the drinking cup an *R*."

Despite the danger, I suddenly felt excited. I picked up the other two blocks, one after the other. "There's a snake and an eagle. I think the snake is an *E* and the eagle a *Y*."

"Grey?" Beatrice said, then I tried all the words together.

"A den so grey? But what does that mean?"

But at that moment, several guards burst into the room beneath us, shouting in Russian.

"What do we do now?" Beatrice cried.

Dr. Drake pointed upwards. "Look to the skies!"

I followed his gaze and felt a surge of relief. "It's Koa!"

In the nick of time, Koa landed on the roof and we scrambled up onto his back. As we gained height I scanned the scene below. By now the fire started by the Tunguska had spread across a good part of the jungle, sending up a pall of black smoke. "What about Torcher?"

I need not have worried, for a moment later we were joined by Idraigir and Erasmus, who had a very smug-looking Torcher riding on his back.

Dr. Drake hailed them. "What happened to the Tunguskas?" he cried.

"They ran into us," replied Idraigir. "And got rather more than they bargained for."

Dr. Drake smiled. "And good riddance to them!" By now we were flying along the ridge that lead to the summit of the volcano. "Koa, set us down over there, please. We need to decide on our next course of action before we go any farther. We daren't risk an engagement with the whole of Alexandra's dragon army."

Koa did as he was bid and we dismounted.

"So, we now have all ten letters of the clue," declared Dr. Drake. "A-D-E-N-S-O-G-R-E-Y. Does that mean anything to you, Koa?"

The amphithere shook his head.

Beatrice scratched her chin. "A den so grey? Most of the rocks around here are black."

"Perhaps the den is the next place we have to look," I suggested. "The place where we have to find the key."

Beatrice frowned. "Unless it's another riddle and we're not supposed to be looking for a real den at all."

Suddenly I had an idea. "What if 'a den so grey' is an anagram?"

"Of course!" said Dr. Drake. He took a stick and

scratched the letters into the dirt on the ground. The three of us stared at them for a while, silently.

Something was troubling me. "I'm not sure that we've got the whole picture," I said. "There's a line in the last clue that I still don't understand. It said, 'Look above to solve this clue, Then watch the master watching you.' But we haven't seen a master at all. Does that mean a Dragon Master? Are we supposed to see a picture of one? Where would we see that?"

I looked at the letters on the ground and had a sudden flash of inspiration. All at once, the letters rearranged themselves in my mind and the answer swam into view. A chill raced through my body. Of course!

"The Dragon's Eye!" I shouted. "The answer to the anagram is 'Dragon's Eye'!"

Even Dr. Drake's seemed impressed as he took the gem from his pocket. "The Dragon's Eye, why, yes, of course. Well done, Daniel! Whoever the Dragon Master is, his image is fixed inside the gem so that he appears to be looking back at you from a mirror. No wonder the Dragon's Eye has always been so important!"

Beatrice let out a low whistle. "Now for the difficult part," she said.

But at that moment, Flitz—who must have followed us all the way from the pyramid complex—appeared, as if from nowhere, and made a swoop for the gem. He would have easily plucked it from Dr. Drake's hand, had it not been for Torcher's lightning reaction. The chick sprang up and knocked Flitz aside, and the dwarf dragon retreated with a bitter roar. Dr. Drake hastily returned the Dragon's Eye to his waistcoat pocket.

"That was close!" Beatrice shuddered and then began to shake her head slowly, as a dreadful realisation dawned. "Oh, my goodness. . . . Maybe that's why Alexandra hasn't made more of an effort to catch us. What if all of this has been planned, right from the very beginning? Perhaps Flitz has been following us all along."

Dr. Drake nodded slowly. "By Jove, Beatrice, you could be right."

I had no idea what they were talking about. Hadn't Torcher just saved the day? "What do you mean?"

"Alexandra knew that she couldn't find the key to the cavern on her own. She's been letting us find it for her! That's why she brought us to the island in the first place," explained Beatrice. "She knows where the hammer is. All she needs now is the Dragon's Eye and she can take possession of it!"

We finally understood the hopelessness of our situation. "So all Flitz has to do is to tell her that we have discovered that the Dragon's Eye is the key, and she will order her dragon army to capture us," I said. "We don't stand a chance."

"We must tarry no longer," declared Koa. "Let us go to

the Cave of Dragons at once. The Dragon Master must be the one to unlock the door, as Beatrice Croke intended."

But as we set off on Koa, something else was troubling me. "There's one thing about this I don't understand. Flitz isn't controlled by dragon dust, is he? He is helping Alexandra, but do you think he has any idea at all what is going to happen to the dragons if Miss Gorynytchka finally gets her hands on the hammer? Won't it burst his heart and kill him, too?"

Dr. Drake looked thoughtful. "I'm sure you are right, Daniel. I don't think that Flitz can have the faintest idea what she is really planning."

"So I wonder what he would do if he found out," I replied.

Chapter Fifteen

THE THIRTEENTH TREASURE

A true student of dragonology doesn't give a FIG for the three
chief enemies of dragonkind: Fear, Ignorance and Greed.

—— *Dr. Ernest Drake, Letters to a Young Dragonologist*

An ominous cloud of black smoke had spread over
the island as Koa flew us to the Cave of Dragons.
I gripped the feathers of his mane tightly, half expecting Alexandra's dragon army to attack, but the skies were
strangely empty. The peak of the volcano was buried under
a carpet of cinders, while the lava had risen to the top of
the crater, where it danced feverishly, throwing occasional
gouts of magma high into the sky. It did not take an expert
to divine that an eruption could happen at any time.

Koa flew us into the gorge and deposited us on the slip-
pery ledge that ran behind the grey cascade. "The Cave of
Dragons lies through there. But remember: fetch only the
hammer and anvil. Leave all else where you find it."

Farther along the ledge was a pair of stone doors, dripping with lichen and moss. Two shining gems, very like the Dragon's Eye, were set into the centre of each door, and the image of a different face had been fixed into each gem. One showed the image of Beatrice Croke, while the other showed an amphithere, who might have been Koa or his brother, Kua. There was a socket for a third gem in between them. Dr. Drake took out the Dragon's Eye and, brushing away some of the moss, placed it into the empty socket. Then, he stood back as a swirl of dragon fire appeared in the heart of each of the three gems. The doors swung inwards to reveal a dark, dry cave, piled high with weapons and glittering treasures. But in the centre, radiating pure evil and hanging by its immense haft above an anvil of black etched glass, was the Hammer of the Dragons itself. Dr. Drake strode into the cave and reached to take it. Judging by its size and the ease with which Dr. Drake plucked it from its place, the hammer was obviously much lighter than it looked.

"And so we take possession of the thirteenth treasure," he said gravely.

I felt at once relieved that we had found the hammer — and terrified at its awful potential. We knew we had to move fast, but before we had even turned to leave the chamber, a voice interrupted us. "Stay!" it commanded us. "The Hammer of the Dragons is mine!"

I spun round to behold Alexandra Gorynytchka, dressed in a cloak and hood so streaked with ashes that she might have been a demon born out of the cinders of the volcano, rather than a flesh-and-blood human. She stood tall in the mouth of the cave, a long finger reaching out in front of her, and her dark eyes flashing under the cinder-grey hood. Flitz was crouched on her shoulder like an imp, and behind her crowded a host of dragons, a few in the doorway, others hovering just beyond the waterfall, and more crisscrossing the brooding skies. But of her human guards there was no sign. Had they fled, fearing the eruption?

Alexandra advanced into the cave. "Give me the hammer, Drake. As you see, you are in no position to refuse me."

"Beware, enemy of dragonkind!" cried Dr. Drake. "I have a weapon; you yourself are unarmed. If I strike a blow, it will finish everything."

"Then strike," said Alexandra.

There was a long pause. The earth gave a shudder and I stumbled. Alexandra Gorynytchka did not react. Instead, she laughed and gestured towards Torcher.

"You will not strike a blow with the hammer," she said. "You are afraid of what will happen to this creature."

Dr. Drake did not respond. Instead, remembering our earlier discussion, he directed his gaze at the dwarf dragon. "I hope that you can understand this, Flitz. You and I may not be on the same side, but I am sworn to be a friend to all dragons. And if your mistress unleashes the power of the hammer, then you, too, will die."

Alexandra laughed. "That is nonsense. Don't listen to their lies, Flitz."

Did I see Flitz shuffle uncertainly? Had he finally understood? But this was no time for conjecture. Beatrice positioned herself between Alexandra and Dr. Drake, and I took up my place beside her.

My sister folded her arms. "The hammer isn't yours," she said. "It belongs to the Secret and Ancient Society of Dragonologists!"

"Beatrice, please," said Dr. Drake. "You must get behind me."

Alexandra flicked back the hood of her cloak so that we could see her cruel face more clearly. She let out a peal of laughter. On her head she wore an outlandish helmet that reminded me of some of the ornate helms I had passed in the treasure vaults of the dragon city. She shook her head. "You should congratulate these children rather than upbraid them, Drake," she said. "Their foolish bravery is to be applauded. Perhaps one of them would have made a good Dragon Master, after all."

"One of us still will," I shouted back, furious.

Alexandra smiled sadly. "I see that even now you children do not understand what is happening. But the time for childish games is over. I expect that Drake has told you that dragons are in some sort of danger of dying out. Do not believe him. They are multiplying. They will rise up. And then where will your precious human civilisation be?"

"Dragons will not rise up. They are our friends." Beatrice's face was red with fury.

"We shall see. Let me make you an offer," said Alexandra. "I know how you both yearn for the power that Drake is too weak to use. Come with me and I shall make you both Dragon Masters. We can share the power of the hammer and learn to use it wisely. Not every dragon needs to die," she asserted breezily. "A judicious cull is all that is required. You can choose which ones should survive. Together we shall usher in a new age of peace between humans and dragons."

"Do you honestly expect Daniel and Beatrice to be taken in by your preposterous lies?" Dr. Drake fumed. The woman was ridiculous, but she was making Dr. Drake angry, and maybe that was part of her plan.

Alexandra's eyes shone with a wicked light. She was enjoying herself. "It is you who is the liar, Drake, making promises to these children that are not in your power to keep, and you know it."

"But you can't make anyone Dragon Master," I cried. "Only the dragons can do that."

Alexandra shook her head. "With the hammer in my possession, I have the power to do anything I choose! The hammer is mine by right, and I have made you an offer that will spare your lives." She paused, pretending to be affronted. "If you are not going to accept it, then stand aside."

Beatrice folded her arms. "I thought you were strong, but now I can see how weak you are. Are you really bound by a curse your ancestor made eight hundred years ago?"

At that, Alexandra laughed out loud. "My ancestor was a pitiful fool. He should have refused to give up the hammer. He should have risen to challenge both King Yaroslav and Harald Hardrada. Instead, he meekly allowed the hammer to be taken from him, and only then made an oath that one day our family would reclaim it. That fool left his heirs to achieve what he, in his cowardice, could not." She snapped her fingers. "That's how much I care for his oath—a fig! The hammer is mine because I say it is mine. So give it to me, or these children shall be slain on the spot."

Alexandra pushed past Beatrice and me, plucked the hammer from Dr. Drake's hands, and, closing her eyes, pressed it to her face.

"At last," she said. "How I have longed for this moment. Now you will see the power of the hammer unleashed. You shall be my witnesses." She turned to the dragons behind her. "Bring them," she said. "And bring the anvil. The moment of my triumph is nigh!"

We made a sorry spectacle, Dr. Drake, Beatrice, and I, on the top of the volcano, surrounded by Alexandra's Tunguskan army, both in the air and on the ground. There was a constant rumbling sound, ash drifted from the dark skies, and the only light was a hellish orange glow from the crater, which grew brighter whenever a spout of lava was flung into the air.

Flitz was nowhere to be seen. Four Tunguskas guarded Torcher. This time there would be no escape. I clutched my sister and Dr. Drake, while Alexandra Gorynytchka stood in front of the crystal anvil, which had been set up a few feet from the crater's edge. How could she stand such incredible heat? She took a few practice swings with the hammer, smiling to think, perhaps, that such an object could dance so easily in her hands.

"Now I will settle my accounts. I have long yearned to see this hammer in action," she said. "Bring me the dragon chick."

Torcher struggled, but he was no match for the Tunguskas, who hauled him towards the anvil.

"They didn't take your dragon whistle, Daniel," hissed Beatrice. "Blow it. Summon Idraigir and Koa. We have to put a stop to this."

My hand went to the chain but stopped halfway. "If I do that, won't they die, too, when Alexandra strikes the hammer against the anvil?"

"The prophecy calls for an army of free dragons to stand up to the army of enslaved dragons," said Beatrice. "We have to believe in it now. It's our only chance."

I put the dragon whistle to my lips, but at first they

trembled so much that I could not make a sound, then finally I managed to blow a note. It was as if they had been waiting for precisely that call, for the black clouds parted for a moment and Koa flew down to perch on the opposite rim of the crater, followed by Idraigir and Erasmus and the rest of our dragon army: Brythonnia and Tregeagle; Panthéon, and a number of gargouilles; Uwassa, and six or seven enormous wyverns. But there were so few of them. So very few. Surely we wouldn't stand a chance if it came to a fight.

"Dragon Master," called Erasmus. "Shall we give the order to attack?"

Alexandra held the hammer above Torcher's head and laughed. "Please, go ahead. Then I shall strike the anvil instead of this dragon chick. You shall all die instantly. Such a shame, as I had thought to let one or two of you live. I was thinking of having my own menagerie of tame dragons."

"Wait, Erasmus," said Dr. Drake.

"Yes, wait, Erasmus," echoed Alexandra mockingly. "I never thought the day would come when I would thank Dr. Ernest Drake for anything, but as it was his interference that brought you all here and saved me the trouble of laboriously slaying you one by one, it would be churlish not to offer him some words of appreciation."

She raised the hammer.

"Take me!" called Idraigir. "Let the chick go, and take me instead."

Alexandra laughed again. "You were one of the ones who I was especially hoping to save, Idraigir," she said. "I was looking forward to seeing you bow down before me each day to receive your orders. But no matter. Come before me now and place your head on the ground."

Dr. Drake stiffened at my side.

I was horrified. "Don't trust her, Idraigir!" I shouted. "It's a trick. She will kill Torcher anyway." But the Guardian Dragon didn't seem to hear me. Behind Alexandra I saw Flitz flying up over the top of the crater to watch from behind his mistress. He couldn't have understood what Dr. Drake had tried to tell him, after all. Now he would die with the rest.

Beatrice gripped my arm so hard that it hurt. "But Idraigir mustn't!" she said.

"There is no alternative," said Dr. Drake. "The prophecy speaks of a sacrifice. It must be made willingly."

Now the noble dragon was kneeling before Alexandra.

"Good," said Alexandra. "Lay your head down here next to the anvil."

Idraigir did as he was told.

"Why doesn't he just blast her with a jet of flame?" asked Beatrice incredulously. "Don't the Tunguskas understand what is happening? She means to kill them, too!"

"I am afraid her power over them is too great," explained Dr. Drake.

"Koa, stop her!" I yelled. "You have to save Idraigir."

But the amphithere remained motionless. Alexandra stepped forwards and raised the hammer with two hands.

"You are a fool, Idraigir," she said. "Do you think that your sacrifice will save the other dragons? Do you think that the deranged prophecy of a drowning shaman is worth any more than my ancestor's oath? You should have listened to Daniel. You have failed. I shall kill them all!"

She raised the hammer over the anvil and I felt myself cry out. She meant to strike the anvil itself—not just Idraigir! Beside me, Beatrice gasped, waiting for the baneful knell that would burst the heart of every dragon within earshot. But it never came. Instead, Alexandra screamed and flailed around with the hammer as she desperately tried to fend off Flitz, who was ripping and clawing at her face. The four Tunguskas who had been guarding Torcher instantly abandoned the dragon chick and swarmed towards the dwarf dragon, but Flitz dodged them and dived back to redouble his feverish attack. Alexandra held the hammer in one hand and tried to land a blow on the anvil, while protecting her face with the other. But it was Idraigir himself who prevented her, by coiling his tail around her waist and dragging her inexorably towards the edge of the crater. She would be burned to a cinder, and good riddance.

But now the four Tunguskas leapt forward to defend her, sinking their teeth into Idraigir's wings and flank. Somehow, Alexandra Gorynytchka proved immune to the searing flames that the Guardian poured over her like water, though she remained in Idraigir's firm grip.

"Flitz!" Alexandra screamed. "Do not believe their lies. Why would I kill you, my loyal and trusted servant? I order you to stop!"

It was not our words, however, that had finally turned Flitz against Alexandra, but her own, and the evidence that he had seen with his own eyes. Out of range of the anvil, Alexandra rained down heavy blows from the hammer on Idraigir, and finally, he keeled over, thick black blood seeping from between his scales and dissolving the very rock that lay beneath it. The scales should have been invulnerable, but they were no match for the might of the hammer. Fearing that the hellish weapon would crush them, too, the Tunguskas released Idraigir and backed out of range. Flitz, however, did not give up. He continued snapping at Idraigir and Alexandra alike in a berserk rage.

"Help me!" screamed Alexandra, struggling to loosen herself from the grip of the dying dragon. The Tunguskas loped unwillingly back into the fray, helping her to wriggle out a little from Idraigir's coils. She flung off the remains of her tattered cloak to reveal that in addition to her Atlantean helmet, she was encased from head to foot—from gauntlets to heavy boots—in thick dragon-hide armour.

"So that is how she withstood the heat at the edge of the crater!" I commented with a grimace. Flitz's teeth left no mark upon it, and the flames that spewed from Idraigir's mouth lapped uselessly against it. And now Idraigir's hold on Alexandra was weakening.

"We have to help him," I cried to Dr. Drake.

The Dragon Master's eyes were damp with grief. "It is too late," he told us quietly. "We cannot help him. His wounds are mortal. Instead we must save the other dragons. . . . We must destroy the hammer."

Torcher roared and leapt forwards gallantly, but Alexandra struck him a glancing blow and he tumbled lifelessly to the ground. Then, lashing out, she hit one of her Tunguskas with the hammer by mistake, knocking it out cold and sending the others into a retreat. She pounded Idraigir's head, causing him to stumble and loosen his grip on her further. Would she be able to reach the anvil after all?

At the last moment, Idraigir, despite his crippling injuries, summoned all his strength, curled his tail around Alexandra's waist once more, and caught Flitz between his jaws. Then he began to drag the vicious pair to the crater's edge, and the three of them teetered on the brink.

As the ground gave way beneath their feet, Flitz broke free of Idraigir in a last bid for freedom. Alexandra, still trapped within Idraigir's coils, realised that there was no hope. She let out an anguished scream and flung the hammer up into the air as high as she could. Her hands free now, she snatched at Flitz and caught the diminutive dragon by the tail. Now all three of them plunged towards the lava,

Idraigir with his eyes held firmly on Dr. Drake, Flitz with a frantic flapping of tiny wings, and Alexandra with a final, chilling shriek.

A moment later, the hammer hit the surface of the magma. It seemed to explode, for within seconds, a fifty-foot jet of lava plumed skywards, before falling back around the crater like fiery rain.

"The volcano!" cried Beatrice, horrified. "It's erupting!"

Chapter Sixteen

THE ERUPTION

*Some places can get too hot even for a dragon
to be truly comfortable.*

—— *Dr. Ernest Drake, Letters to a Young Dragonologist*

The eruption was immense; huge chunks of rock collapsed into the lava lake, which was bubbling up over the top of the crater wall, and the ground around us shuddered and danced as though the volcano had become detached from its very root. Vast cracks opened at our feet, while the sky was filled with a dark cloud of dragons hurrying to escape. Many of the Tunguskas glanced around wildly, not knowing what to do next.

"Come on, Bea." I grabbed my sister's hand and we raced down the slope to where Dr. Drake was waiting with Koa and Tregeagle. We stumbled towards them over the hot ash, covering our mouths as best we could. Beatrice tripped and I helped her up just as a fiery boulder crashed to the ground in front of us, missing Torcher by inches. Another rock exploded into a thousand pieces behind us, and Beatrice let out a scream. I froze. Where were they coming from? Above us, the shapes of dragons hovered, their outlines darker than the black smoke.

"The Tunguskas are still trying to kill us!" I cried. Another boulder came crashing down, and then another. But there was no castle to protect us this time; it would be only a matter of a few short moments before one of us would be burned or crushed. By now the smoke belching from the volcano had thickened into a flaming column, while the ground underneath us felt like the deck of a ship in a rough sea. Koa, Tregeagle, and Brythonnia were flying up to confront the Tunguskas, and the sky emptied of hurtling boulders as the two sides clashed. Beatrice and I clung to each other for support as we fled, with Torcher, towards Dr. Drake.

"Why are they trying to kill us?" I gasped as we reached him, gesturing up at the Tunguskas.

"Alexandra's influence will not disappear at once. It will take time for the effects of the dragon dust to wear off. We must get away from this place." Lava had crested the lip of the crater and was starting to flow, slowly but surely, in our direction. But in a few moments, as it reached the steeper slope above us, it would pick up speed and we would be finished.

"Where's Erasmus?" I cried. The white dragon was

usually impossible to miss. We scanned the sky above our heads; the battle was not going well for our dragon army. Several of our bravest dragons — Tregeagle among them — had fallen to the ground, and even the mighty wyvern Uwassa was showing signs of weakening as he fought ten or twenty Tunguskas amid a mass of wings, tails, and flames.

One Tunguska broke away from the melee and flew towards us, breathing out a jet of flame. Torcher leapt to our defence, baring his teeth and spreading out his wings as a fireproof barrier to deflect the fire. The Tunguska came in low and nearly took my head off with a lunge from its claw. Then another two black dragons headed towards us. One swooped down, picking up a boulder.

"Over there!" shouted Dr. Drake, pointing to a rocky outcrop.

We scrambled farther away from the lava flow, but the Tunguskas were right behind us. I turned and saw that two more had caught up with us, one aiming its heavy arrow-head tail at Dr. Drake, the other diving towards me with fire on its lips. I had nowhere to run. I was caught between a sheer drop on one side, and lava on the other. I began preparing myself for the worst.

But suddenly a magnificent white creature flew up over the ridge, and I felt a rush of icy air as it spewed out a frosty blast that met the Tunguska's flame in midair.

"It's the frost dragons!" cried Beatrice. "Erasmus has

fetched the frost dragons! And he must have done something to them; they aren't hypnotised anymore!"

The Tunguskas corkscrewed away from us to face the new threat. A roar that sounded like a cheer went up from the dragons on our side.

"Good old Erasmus!" I shouted, my voice quavering. I should have known all along that he would never let us down. Already some of the Tunguskas must have sensed that things were not going their way, for out of the corner of my eye, I saw them flying away.

"Quickly!" cried Erasmus as he landed with two other frost dragons. "Koa says that the whole island is going to explode. These are my cousins, Nuki and Tok. Alexandra's human helpers fled the island some time ago, so all I had to do was free them from their chains. Climb on. Bring Torcher. And cover your ears."

Dr. Drake climbed up onto Erasmus, while I got onto Nuki with Torcher, and Beatrice onto Tok. We took off. The dragons had ceased fighting now, though we could still sense the tension in the air as we sped away from the doomed island, our dragons flying as fast as their wings could carry them.

Nervously, I looked back. The top of the volcano was lit up with an ever-expanding bulb of white magma. Then came a deafening explosion as the entire peak burst upwards into the sky. A few seconds later, a shock wave of blistering heat blew over me, and Nuki lost control for a moment, rolling over and over so that Torcher and I grasped desperately at his white scales. Parts of the sea were already boiling where they had been struck by molten debris, and the sky was teeming with dragons, fleeing the devastation.

The frost dragons were flying together in formation behind their leader. Tregeagle was flying with us, so he had escaped, at least, but where were Erasmus and Dr. Drake? Had they gone back to check for survivors? By now what was left of the volcano—which was rapidly receding into the distance—had disappeared under a smoking wave of lava and ash that was swallowing up the lower slopes at a ferocious speed.

Far below us a little ship bobbed up and down on the seawater. It seemed hardly to be moving, but from the plume of smoke billowing out horizontally from its chimneys, I could see it was racing away from the island as fast as it could.

"Look," I shouted across to Beatrice, pointing down at them. "Those must be Alexandra's men."

"They were lucky to get away," she replied.

Suddenly there came another explosion. I winced and clutched my hands to my ears. It was louder than any sound I had ever heard. I looked around, and the entire Island of Dragons had vanished, but for a cloud of steam, rising from the ocean, and a wave, ten times the size of the tallest wyvern, racing across the sea. The men on the ship were going to be in trouble.

There was still no sign of Erasmus and Dr. Drake. A huge black ring of smoke was spreading out behind me, from where the island had once been. Surely no one could have survived such an explosion. My heart gave a heavy, desperate thud. But just as I was finally giving up all hope, the frost dragon burst through the cloud with Dr. Drake, a tiny black dot on his brilliant white back and Koa flying steadily alongside him. They were outpacing even the aftermath of the disaster on their swift dragon wings. As they neared us, Dr. Drake waved wildly and Beatrice and I waved back, with tears of relief pouring down our cheeks.

Being Arctic-Antarctic migrators, frost dragons are used to flying for days at a time, but after our ordeal it was not long before Beatrice and I were suffering from hunger and thirst. Dr. Drake must have felt the same way, for he leaned forwards and whispered something to Erasmus that I could not catch. The young dragon called out to Nuki and Tok, and they left the formation and followed him. A few hours later we reached land, flying over a desert until the dragons set us down near a city, which Dr. Drake informed us was Marrakesh, in Morocco. We humans walked into town, and Dr. Drake raised some funds by selling the golden chain from which the Dragon's Eye usually hung. After a trip to the public baths, we ate a hearty meal in a large market square before making several purchases of warm clothing and rugs. We returned to the dragons and used the rugs first as sleeping blankets and then as makeshift dragon saddles, so that our onward journey would be more comfortable.

It was dusk the next day when we landed on the lawn of Castle Drake. The news of the battle had spread, and Mother and Father were waiting for us, along with our friend Darcy and Mademoiselle Gamay, Dr. Drake's housekeeper.

We greeted Mademoiselle Gamay and Darcy warmly and hugged our parents, but when I started to tell them what had happened, Dr. Drake held up his hand.

"I think that we had best take our leave of the dragons before your parents hear the full story of our adventures. Nuki and Tok are famished, and we would be showing terrible ingratitude if we kept them from the Arctic any longer than necessary."

We thanked the frost dragons profusely, and Erasmus stepped forwards.

"If you adult humans don't mind, I would like to have a word with Daniel and Beatrice in private."

Intrigued, we followed him around the side of Castle Drake to the coal shed, where we had first kept Scorcher and had hatched out Torcher's egg and given him his first — unwelcome — bath. The shed had been rebuilt, but it still bore scorch marks from the time when it had nearly burned down.

"I must take my leave of you," said Erasmus. "But you two will always have my heartfelt thanks for everything you have done for dragonkind. Your actions will not be forgotten. If you are ever in danger and a dragon can help you, your great deeds will be remembered. Isn't that right, Torcher?"

The dragon chick, who had come looking for us, gazed up at Erasmus and put his head on one side. We laughed.

"Are you going with Nuki and Tok, then?" asked Beatrice.

"I think so, yes. It has been too long since I have visited the land of the midnight sun, and there are things now afoot in the world of dragons that cannot wait."

"But we will see you again in Scotland, won't we?" I said hopefully.

"I am afraid not," Erasmus answered gravely. "I have enjoyed the challenge of learning about humans. It has, to my surprise, been a very great pleasure. It is a memory that I shall cherish. But my studies have come to an end. I am no longer Idraigir's apprentice."

Of course! I thought back to Idraigir's tragic and noble sacrifice, and it dawned on me for the first time the consequences his actions would have on Erasmus. Our dragon tutor would become the new Guardian. I hoped we would be invited to Wharncliffe for the ceremony, but it seemed inappropriate to ask just now. First there would need to be a memorial ceremony for Idraigir.

"Will you appoint another dragon to help us study?" asked Beatrice.

Erasmus looked at us with sad eyes. "That is what I

wanted to talk to you about. I am afraid that things cannot be the way they were before. You two have shown more aptitude for dragonology than any other humans I have ever met—even more, perhaps, than Dr. Drake. You have shown patience, bravery, resilience, and good humour. And if there were more humans like you in the world, I would consider it. But, sadly, most humans are not like you."

"What do you mean?" I blurted out desperately. "What about our dragonological studies? We can try harder."

"It is not a question of trying harder. It is a question of what is best for both our species. The fact is that the time has come for dragons and humans to sever ties and go their separate ways."

"Sever ties? W-w-why?" I stammered. After all we had been through together, I could hardly believe what Erasmus was saying.

"Because there are too many humans in this world, and too few dragons," Erasmus replied calmly. "Events of the last few years have shown us that even with humans such as Dr. Drake and yourselves to help us, we dragons continue to be in great danger. It will be safest for us if we simply disappear. If we seem not to exist, then there will be no secrets to give away."

I shook my head. I could not believe it. "Forever?"

"Maybe not forever. But for a very long time."

Beatrice looked at the dragon chick. "What about Torcher?" she asked fearfully.

"Torcher too." Erasmus nodded. "He must return to the wild."

My sister turned pale and looked at our little dragon, who seemed unaware of the conversation going on around him. "When?" she whispered.

"Soon," Erasmus answered, his voice a little gentler now. "Even though you love him, Torcher is not a pet. He is a wild dragon. You have raised him well. And lately he has shown that although he is still an infant, he can nearly fly, and he is more than capable of looking after himself."

I was devastated but tried to stay calm. "Does Dr. Drake know?"

Erasmus nodded again. "He and I have discussed it at length. But do not be angry with him. He thought that Torcher should just disappear, that the quick, hard way would be the easiest in the end. But I am going to let you spend one final month with him, here in the forest. I believe that is the least you deserve after all you have been through. Idraigir is not the only one who has had to make sacrifices."

"Thank you," said Beatrice. We both hung our heads.

"You should have a moment of triumph, and I wish that this would not lessen your enjoyment of that moment, though I fear it will." Erasmus straightened and I could see that he was preparing to leave.

I smiled, although my heart was broken, and held out my hand. "Do not worry, Erasmus. You are doing what you believe is best." I gulped back the lump in my throat. "Farewell. Until we see you again."

Erasmus took my hand in his huge claw. "Farewell, Daniel. We will meet again one last time, a month from now, when humans and dragons gather for a final ceremony in memory of Idraigir."

And with that he took off, leaving Beatrice and me gazing at our beloved dragon chick in sorrow and disbelief.

The next few weeks back in our home in St. Leonard's Forest passed all too quickly. We spent every moment we could with Torcher. He was developing new skills all the time, and he had even started to understand English quite well. We watched him hunt, and bring new things that he had found back to his lair. He was learning to fly, and sometimes we sent him out into the forest so that we could track him, but always with a sense of sadness and the knowledge that times like these would not come again. Although he didn't know exactly what Erasmus had told us, Torcher seemed to know that something was wrong, for he would sometimes sit and simply look at us, as though trying to reassure us that he would never forget us.

"Don't worry, Torcher," said Beatrice one day, when Torcher had refused to move very far from the house. "We'll come to visit you wherever you are."

We had our record books open on the lawn and Torcher

had come to join us, lying down between us. We were trying to write up our adventures so as not to forget them.

"You certainly showed Flitz, didn't you, old fellow?" I said.

"Poor Flitz, though," said Beatrice.

"Poor Flitz, my eye," I scoffed. "He was one of the few dragons that wasn't hypnotised. He could have left Alexandra anytime he liked."

Beatrice looked at me in consternation. "He still didn't deserve his fate, though. Did he, Torcher?"

But from the way Torcher bared his teeth, I am not so sure that he agreed. He was a wild dragon, after all.

"We're going to miss you when you return to the wild, Torcher," I said with a rueful laugh. "Are you going to miss us, too?"

Torcher didn't answer but instead raced off to his lair, returning a few minutes later with something in his mouth. He bent down and dropped two small objects between Beatrice and me. They were a piece of flint and a piece of iron pyrites. I looked at them in amazement.

"By Jove!" I exclaimed. "I recognise these! They're were the ones that you stole from my pocket, Torcher. Are you giving them back to us as a keepsake?"

Torcher pushed them towards us with his snout.

"But if you do that, how are you going to breathe fire?"

In answer, Torcher lifted up his head and let out a rich stream of flame.

Beatrice laughed. "He's found other ones, of course, haven't you, Torcher?"

"Then we'll take one each, won't we, Beatrice," I said, passing her the iron pyrites and slipping the flint into my pocket.

The next morning, I lingered with Father over breakfast. Suddenly, Beatrice came running back to the house with tears streaming down her face. "It's happened," she said. "Torcher has gone."

"But he didn't even say good-bye!" I exclaimed.

Beatrice rushed over to the table and put her arm around my shoulder. "I think he did, Daniel. He said it yesterday."

I pulled the flint from my pocket and gazed at it despondently.

"Well, I suppose," I said at last, trying to smile a little, "things aren't as bad as they seem. When we find out where he has gone to live we can go to visit him."

Father put down his newspaper abruptly. "I'm sorry, Daniel. I am afraid that none of us will ever know where he is living."

"Not even Dr. Drake?" Surely the Dragon Master would be kept informed.

"Not even Dr. Drake."

"You mean that we're never going to see him again, ever?" said Beatrice.

"Don't worry," said Mother. "You will see him at the memorial. You will be able to say good-bye again then, if you wish." And, trying to sound cheery, she held up a letter. "This came this morning," she said. "It is from Lord Chiddingfold on behalf of the Society of Dragons. The memorial for Idraigir will take place in one week's time. We are all invited." But her voice wobbled at the mention of the ceremony, and we knew at once that she was upset, too.

I took the letter. The last communication that we'd had from the Society of Dragons had been on a piece of dragon skin, and the lettering had faded even as I read it. This, however, was simply written on a piece of notepaper.

"It will be the very final meeting of the Secret and Ancient Society of Dragonologists," said Father. "In deference to the wishes of the dragons, now that Alexandra Gorynytchka has been defeated, it has been decided that the active part of the S.A.S.D. should be disbanded."

"Disbanded?" I could hardly believe it.

"It is for the best," said Father. "After all, if nobody knows about dragons, then they aren't going to bother them, are they? The secret of their existence will truly be safe."

"But what are you and Mother going to do?" asked Beatrice.

"Well, we have found positions that we think will suit our particular skills. We're going to work for the British Museum as dinosaur collectors. Any number of fossils have been found recently in Sussex, and the museum would like us to dedicate our time to cataloguing them and searching for new specimens."

"Oh," I said. It sounded exciting, but it was hardly the same as studying dragons.

That night I found Beatrice standing in Torcher's empty lair, surveying the small room that had once been his home. "Where do you think he's gone?" she said bravely.

"Somewhere mountainous," I said. "Fully grown, he would have been too big for this forest, that's for sure."

She pointed to a small brazier in the corner. "To think that we kept his egg warm on that, back at Castle Drake."

I smiled weakly. "Do you remember when I gave him his first bath?"

"I think you got considerably wetter than he did." Beatrice laughed, but her eyes were wet and shining. "And remember what a liability he was all the way to Jaisalmer."

"He came in useful for lighting fires, though, didn't he?" I said.

My sister nodded. "He grew up so quickly. This time it was Torcher who saved us, wasn't it? It used to be us who saved him."

Beatrice was right. I supposed we could not have kept Torcher much longer, whatever the situation, but not seeing him again was going to be so hard. "I wonder if Erasmus will make a speech when he is made Guardian," I said.

"Well, very soon we're going to find out," said Beatrice, and she put her arm around me as we walked back to the house.

CHAPTER SEVENTEEN
THE JUDGEMENT
OF ERASMUS

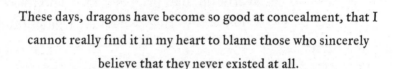

These days, dragons have become so good at concealment, that I
cannot really find it in my heart to blame those who sincerely
believe that they never existed at all.

—— *Dr. Ernest Drake, Letters to a Young Dragonologist*

To my surprise, Idraigir's memorial was not to be held
in Wharncliffe, but at his lair high on the mountain of
Cader Idris, in Wales. We travelled to the town of Dolgellau,
which was closest to the mountain, in a coach with Darcy
and our old friends Billy and Alicia, the son and daughter of
Lord Chiddingfold. Billy told us the dramatic, but not alto-
gether unexpected, news that the government had, on Lord
Chiddingfold's own recommendation, decided to shelve the
post of Minister for Dragons for the foreseeable future.

"And I must say I'm a bit peeved about it," said Billy,
sounding exasperated. I knew why, and I sympathised. The
Ministry of Dragons, being a secret part of the government,

had been in his family for at least a hundred years, and he had always expected to become Minister himself one day.

"What about Queen Victoria?" asked Beatrice. "She told us she was interested in dragons; she said she wanted to hear more of our adventures."

"The queen has made it clear that she, too, believes this to be the right course of action," replied Alicia.

Everything we had known was changing. And all our hopes and expectations for the future seemed dashed now. But it was the same for everyone we had known and worked with through the S.A.S.D. "What's your father going to do?" I asked.

"Well, it may sound a bit outlandish," Alicia replied, with a bit of a giggle, "but he and Mr. Tibbs have decided to leave politics and invest their time and money in researching heavier-than-air flight. There are some experiments being conducted in France and America that suggest that it might be possible to construct a winged machine that can fly. My father believes that with all of the flying experience he can call on from the S.A.S.D. members, he can get ahead of the competition. After all, if the other great powers are going to have flying machines, we can hardly be left behind, can we?"

"And what about you, Alicia?" asked Beatrice.

"Oh, I'm planning on becoming the first woman pilot, of course," said Alicia breezily.

Upon arrival in Dolgellau, Beatrice and I were in for a surprise, for who should we meet as we walked to our lodgings, but Noah and Nia Hayes, accompanied by the French dragonologist Bernard Gamay and Dr. Drake's housekeeper, Mademoiselle Gamay.

Nia had been a great help to us when we had travelled to China to find a cure for Alexandra's dragon plague; she and her father ran a secret dragon orphanage in Texas.

"So, what are you doing here?" I asked after we had said our hellos.

"You don't have to be any kind of detective to work that out," said Nia. "We're paying our respects to Idraigir."

"And how is the dragon orphanage going?" asked my sister.

"Oh, mighty fine, but I dare say we won't have so many sick dragons to stay now that Miss Gorynytchka is no more."

"What about you, Bernard?" I asked.

"I am well," he replied. "As is Panthéon. You will see him shortly. He is staying with a small group of gargouilles in one of the ruined towers at Harlech Castle. You will be pleased to know that the gargouilles of Paris have finally for-gotten their differences. With Panthéon at their head, they have decided that they can live alongside one another, after all. But one moment, isn't that Miss Ta crossing the road?"

Bernard was right. We had met Miss Ta in China; she was a friend of the Master of Hong Wei Temple and a world expert on Asian *lung* dragons. We had learned a great deal from her on our way home after defeating Alexandra, for the first time, at the Battle of Hong Wei.

"Is the Master coming?" I asked her.

She shook her head.

"He was not well enough to undertake such a long voyage. But he sends his regards and he says, rather cryptically, I must admit, that all things have their own place under heaven, and that the wise man always follows the most natural path." She laughed. "But it is so good to see you," she said, squeezing our hands. "I have very fond memories of you two."

That evening, a grand torch-lit procession—led by Dr. Drake—set out from the town and made its way through starlit fields and along the path that led to the summit of Cader Idris. What the townsfolk made of it, I do not know, but Father told us that Mr. Tibbs had spread a rumour to the effect that we were druids and that it would be best for all and sundry to stay indoors or face dire consequences. So far I had not seen any dragons, and when I did I froze, for there were five of them waiting at the top of the next slope—they were black and I recognised their type only too well.

"Tunguskas!" I cried. "What are they doing here?"

Dr. Drake put a calming hand on my shoulder. "Don't worry, Daniel. They are not going to attack," he said. "They have come to pay their respects. Without Idraigir, they would still be slaves."

I sidled past the Tunguskas, still wary of them, despite Dr. Drake's reassurances. Nevertheless, they fell in calmly and silently behind us at the very back of the procession. Then, a short distance farther on, I spotted the dragon that I wanted to see most of all. Beatrice had seen him, too.

"Torcher!" I cried. "It's Torcher!"

Torcher trotted over to us, licked our faces, and let out a roar that summoned his mother and his brother to our side.

"Scramasax and Scorcher!" exclaimed Beatrice. "It is good to see the two of you. How are you now, Scramasax?"

"I am pleased to say that I have recovered from my grievous wounds at last," said Scramasax. "Which is just as well, as I would not have liked my children to have to attend this sad memorial alone." She looked at us earnestly. "Whatever happens, I would like to say that we dragons are very grateful for all you have done for us. Your good deeds will not be forgotten."

The procession continued and I did not see Erasmus, though I picked out Nuki and Tok from a group of frost dragons. They bowed low as we passed them, then fell in behind us. We passed Panthéon and a group of gargouilles, several *lung,* one of whom I recognised from the battle of Hong Wei, and a number of wyverns. I was sad that Jamal, the young dragon who had flown us all the way to Africa, was not there, but Uwassa was standing by the path and nodded gravely as we passed.

We were very nearly at the top of the mountain. The procession left the main path and headed round a crag. Ahead of us was a cave entrance, and standing in front of it were the noble dragons of the council, Brythonnia, Tregeagle, Somerled, and Ambrosius. Scramasax took her place among them and then—prompted by Dr. Drake, who stood next to Lord Chiddingfold, and Mr. Tibbs, who gave us a nod—we joined the group and waited in silence.

"Where's Erasmus?" I whispered to Mother, who was standing next to us, but she hushed me.

"We are waiting for Koa," said Father under his breath. "He has to arrive before we can begin." I followed his gaze up to the small black dot in the sky that was growing swiftly larger.

At last the amphithere wheeled close and landed gracefully. He was carrying a bag in his mouth, which he passed to Dr. Drake.

"My dragon diaries!" he exclaimed with great delight as he held one up. "I feared that these were lost forever."

"I thought you would like to have them, so I rescued them from the pyramid when the volcano exploded," said Koa. "I meant to give them to you before, but it slipped my mind."

"Thank you, my friend," said Dr. Drake. "As you know, I prize these above gold and silver."

Koa nodded. "My brother felt very much the same about *Liber Draconis.*" A murmur ran through the crowd, and Koa looked around. He cleared his throat. "Now, if I am not mistaken, it is time for us to welcome Erasmus. I believe he has something important to say to us."

Erasmus stepped from the mouth of Idraigir's lair. He gave a roar and began speaking, first in Dragonish and then in English.

"Greetings to you all, both human and dragon," he said. "We are gathered here in front of this cave in order to remember several important things and to make one important judgement. Firstly, we must remember the noble Guardian Idraigir, his eternal vigilance in the war against evil, and the pact that he championed between men and dragons. He died defending us all, and so it is beholden to us all to honour the sacrifice that he made."

At this the assembled dragons roared their approval.

Erasmus continued. "Throughout our long history it has not been usual for dragons and humans to mingle. Dragons are secretive and solitary creatures and prefer to keep to themselves. But since the darkest days during the time of Dragonsbane there has been a Guardian Dragon, and there have been successive Dragon Masters, following in the footsteps of Beatrice Croke. Their job has been to keep secret the existence of dragons, and to keep dragons safe. We thank them and we honour them. We thank the Secret and Ancient Society of Dragonologists for keeping the ancient treasures and for keeping a vigil against an evil that was prophesied long ago. But those tasks are now fulfilled. Therefore, as the head of the Society of Dragons I make this solemn judgement: from this day forward, the

Society of Dragons will cease to exist; there will be no more Guardians."

At this a gasp went up from among the humans, although I guessed that more than half of them had been expecting the news.

"And all the members of the Society are in agreement with me," roared Erasmus. "Beatrice Croke's work is done. The heirs of Dragonsbane have been defeated. The prophecy has been fulfilled, although at greater cost than we had bargained for.

"There are too many humans in the world, and so we dragons are agreed: we must become a secret species once more and hope that humans will forget us. We are becoming scarce, and as the human population of the world grows, we will surely diminish, whatever others may claim."

Erasmus paused to let the full effect of his words sink in.

"Let it be clearly understood," he continued. "With the destruction of the Hammer of the Dragons and the disbanding of the Society of Dragons, there is no longer a need for a Dragon Master, as we are severing all ties with humans. Dr. Ernest Drake, our beloved friend and ally, shall be the last ever Dragon Master. Any who follow us or try to study us do so at their own risk."

Erasmus looked at Beatrice and me with great sadness in his eyes.

"So must it be, my friends," he said. There was a lump in

my throat, and I guessed Beatrice felt the same. She clutched my hand.

"Don't worry, Daniel," she whispered. "It will be all right."

I squeezed her hand back. "I know," I said, though my chin was wobbling now.

"So is it all over?" I asked Dr. Drake when we had said good-bye to Torcher for the last time and started along the path back to our lodgings.

"It is . . ." said Dr. Drake. "And it is not. One adventure ceases, only for another to begin."

"What adventure is that?" asked Beatrice, suddenly hopeful.

"Ah, if I knew, it wouldn't be an adventure, would it?" Dr. Drake replied enigmatically.

"But what will you do?" I asked.

Dr. Drake smiled. "I cannot let this wealth of dragonological knowledge, built up over centuries, disappear forever," he said. "And even if that knowledge is not needed now, who knows what may happen in a hundred years or so? I shall make it the remainder of my life's work to record what I know of dragons, in secret. For now, that body of knowledge shall be available to only a select few, but in the future, who knows? Perhaps one day many will come to read my words and to learn about dragonology."

"Can we still visit you, Dr. Drake?" Beatrice pleaded.

"Of course." He laughed. "Every day, if you like. You now have your own bank of dragonological experience, and that will be useful in my writings, too."

I smiled, relieved that at least we would still have the chance to talk of our experiences from time to time.

"What will happen to Idraigir's cave?" said Beatrice.

"Oh, I imagine that it will be sealed up forever," replied Dr. Drake matter-of-factly.

"And Dr. Drake's Dragonalia?" I asked.

There was a twinkle in Dr. Drake's eye. "Yes, why not?" he said. "I think I shall keep my little shop open."

Farther along the path, Alicia and Billy, Nia, Darcy, and Miss Ta were huddled together, engrossed in conversation. I felt a rush of warmth towards them all, and for the adventures we had shared together, and a sadness, too, that it was all coming to an end.

Dr. Drake saw my expression. "I daresay you and your friends have a great deal to talk about. And I must bid a last farewell to Erasmus." A few moments later, he was gone.

EPILOGUE

Many years have passed since I first met Dr. Drake. I am an old man now. Although Beatrice and I continued to study dragons, of course, I never became Dragon Master. Since that day on Cader Idris, it has become almost impossible to track dragons in the wild. They have deliberately withdrawn from contact with humans, so that now people doubt their very existence. I know that would make the dragons happy. Dr. Drake wrote a great many books about dragons for the students who would come after him; there will never be another such as he to guide them.

As for myself, after that fateful day outside Idraigir's cave I have seen only three dragons. I once caught sight of Weasel running through the forest: I had presumed she must have moved away, but she had simply moved her lair to another, secret location. In March 1899, during the time of the frost dragon migration, I spied a frost dragon flying so high it was almost out of sight. I could have sworn it was Tok.

The third sighting was on July 10, 1918, during the Great War. I remember the date well, for it was on that day that I very nearly lost my life.

Beatrice and I, though middle-aged by now, had each determined to play our part during the war, and she had temporarily given up her job at the British Museum and taken up a post in a munitions factory in Sheffield. Thanks to my love of dragon flying, I had trained as a pilot, and when war broke out, I had been drafted into the Royal Air Corps. Before leaving on a commission in France, I had gone with Beatrice to pay my respects to the old Dragon Master. He had pressed my hand, wished me luck, and shown me some of the many books he had been writing.

Now, on my twentieth mission, I was nursing my Sopwith plane back to base, its fuel tank almost empty. I remember thinking how fuel had never been a problem on the many dragon flights I had made. Suddenly, something jerked me out of my reverie and back into the real world. I heard a distinctive drone and realised that a German Dreidecker fighter plane was bearing down on me out of the summer sky. But though I looked all around, I could not see it at all.

With shocking precision, a line of machine-gun bullets peppered my Sopwith, shattering its wing struts and puncturing holes in its tail fin. Now I knew where my enemy was: he had positioned his aircraft with his back to the setting sun, and the deadly accuracy of his gunnery had damaged my plane so badly that black smoke was pouring from its engine. At any moment I would spin out of control into a final, deadly dive. I swallowed hard. If he hit me again, my chances were nil. My gun was jammed and my enemy knew it. There would be no chivalry, no limping from the field to fight another day; victory would be all his.

In that moment, when death seemed assured, my mind flew back to quite a different time; a time of innocence and wonder. I was standing once more in the basement of a curious shop near the Seven Dials in London, peering through a keyhole and watching a small dragon swooping around and around a laboratory.

My enemy's guns chattered again and my rudder was gone. I shook myself out of the reverie. Next time he would take out the fuel tank. I readied myself, though I knew I stood little chance against him. This time, I told myself, it really was the end.

Then, all at once, something appeared in the sky, like a red pupil in the orange eye of the sun. My enemy veered away from it as though it were a thousand-strong squadron. I saw a jet of flame, leathery wings spread wide, and an arrowhead tail threshing through the sky. A dragon! My heart quickened, and I almost cheered with delight. But what was it doing here, in the middle of a battle? Was it a mirage? Was Death teasing me?

Overcoming his fears now, the German ace turned his plane to face the new threat, and he let fire a hail of bullets. They ricocheted harmlessly off the dragon's flanks. I could imagine how the pilot's face would turn from triumph to consternation, for no matter what he tried, the dragon, which was twice the length of his plane, twisted and turned through the air after him, and he could not escape. The Dreidecker became the prey, clawed and bitten and consumed by fire.

A few moments later a grey parachute opened, and the German pilot floated down towards the waiting troops below. From the markings on their vehicles, I could tell that they were our boys. I grinned to myself. He would spend the rest of the war in captivity.

Meanwhile, the dragon took the top wing of my mangled aircraft in his mouth and gently guided me to a safe landing in the nearest clearing. He sank down next to the plane, the last rays of the disappearing sun glistening along his scales. How he had realised I was in trouble, I'll never know, but we looked at each other, that dragon and I, for a long, silent moment.

"*Praisich boyar,* Torcher!" I cried at last, breaking the spell, but bursting with joy and gratitude.

"*Praisich!*" he cried back. "*Praisich hoyari!*" His voice, thundering as he rose to his feet, let out a final, fiery roar and vanished forever into the dwindling light.

—Daniel Cook, St. Leonard's Forest, 1950